THE ILLUSIONIST

THE ILLUSIONIST

BY FRANÇOISE MALLET-JORIS

INTRODUCTION BY TERRY CASTLE

INTRODUCTION

Even now, half a century after its first publication in 1952, it is hard not to be shocked by *The Illusionist*—the erotically charged story of a lesbian affair between an adolescent French girl living in a small provincial town and her wealthy father's thirty-five-year-old mistress. It's a cold, brilliant, almost reptilian work; the fact that its author, the Franco-Belgian novelist Françoise Mallet-Joris (b. 1930), wrote it at the age of nineteen makes it all the more disconcerting. Even in the sex-obsessed media-world of the twenty-first century such precociousness can be unnerving.

Which isn't to say that *The Illusionist* was, for its time, entirely groundbreaking or indeed especially graphic. True, when it was first published in France—under the title *Le Rempart des Béguines*—critics marveled at the daring subject and praised Mallet-Joris for the skill with which she handled it. (The book was her first: she went on to write twenty more novels and pursue a distinguished career in the 1970s and 1980s as an actress, screenwriter, and songwriter. She was elected to the Académie Goncourt in 1971.) "One shudders to think of the risk of vulgarity which the treatment of such a theme runs," one reviewer wrote; yet such was Mallet-Joris's "astounding maturity," he thought, the book could hardly be called prurient.

No doubt some of the enthusiasm was due to Mallet-Joris's uncanny writerly gifts: even in translation she shines forth, like her countryman Simenon, as a born storyteller. But other factors contributed too. The time was right for such a story. The *éducation sentimentale* has always been a talismanic theme in French literature. Yet before 1950 few writers had addressed it with any real frankness from the female point of view. Colette (1873–1954) was the magnificent exception, of course, and one finds traces of her influence—worldly, subtle, liberating—throughout *The Illusionist*. (Hélène—Mallet-Joris's sly, cynical, profoundly vulnerable narrator—bears an unmistakable resemblance, for example, to Colette's rebellious young heroine, Claudine.) Though Mallet-Joris may not be as well known as de Beauvoir, Duras, Violette Leduc, or indeed Françoise Sagan—whose bestselling *Bonjour, Tristesse* appeared the same year as *The Illusionist* and tells a similar tale of sex and treachery—she was in fact part of that pathbreaking generation of postwar women writers who both embraced the great Colettian theme—erotic self-discovery—and went on to revitalize French literature, theater, cinema, and television in the later 1950s and 1960s.

The topic of female homosexuality was likewise familiar—almost routine—for French-speaking readers. From Laclos, Diderot, and the Marquis de Sade in the eighteenth century through to Balzac, Gautier, Baudelaire, Zola, Maupassant, Proust, Sartre, Genet, and (again) Colette in more modern times, French writers have always had a special purchase on the lesbian theme. From one angle *The Illusionist* is simply part of a larger, often frankly libertine, sapphic tradition in French letters. That Mallet-Joris, even as a teenager, knew the tradition well is clear: at several points in *The Illusionist* she makes reference to it—as if to lay claim, precisely, to a similar knowingness and freedom.

Witness an instance from early in the novel. Not long after Hélène begins her doomed affair with Tamara Soulerr—her widowed father's bisexual Russian mistress—the older woman insists that she read Choderlos de Laclos's *Les Liaisons Dangereuses* (1782), the very title of which is now (as it was in the 1950s) a catchphrase for erotic manipulation and deceit. Tamara's goal at this stage would seem to be to disabuse her young lover of any illusions about life, sex, and desire she might be harboring. But the recommendation is also a vital early clue to Tamara's character. Like the amoral Madame de Merteuil (whose offhand seduction of younger women gives *Les Liaisons* much of its matchless moral horror), Tamara's real interest lies in exploiting her fifteen-year-old protégée for her own narcissistic purposes. She is a born sadist and sex is her weapon of choice. The precocious Hélène—intelligent, bored, yet all too easily enthralled—is hardly impervious. "The book...had an effect I considered wholesome," she observes afterward.

[It] liberated me from a Werther-like sentimentality to which my Germanic origins inclined me all too strongly. Had I followed my own inclinations I would have treasured souvenirs—bits of ribbon, half-smoked cigarettes—and would have looked at a star each night at the same time as did my beloved. Tamara took a high hand with such budding sentimentality, demonstrating its absurdity.

The Laclos novel is part of Hélène's "sentimental education," in other words, one of her lover's many instruments of seduction, but Mallet-Joris also uses it as a signpost—as portent of the evil that is to come.

Elsewhere in the novel Mallet-Joris mines various French sapphic classics for gritty local color—notably the works of Zola and

Maupassant. Toward the end, when their affair has begun to unravel into scenes of outright violence and brutality, Tamara takes Hélène to Lucy's, a squalid lesbian bar in a nearby town. There, as a sort of cruel joke, she forces her lover to dance with Mademoiselle Puck, the place's raddled and foul-mouthed proprietress. Down to the dizzying fug of alcohol, perfume, and sweat, the press of swaying and drunken women, the "shrill cries sounding from tables," Mallet-Joris seems to have borrowed many of her details from a similar scene in Zola's *Nana* (1880).

Yet while such allusions no doubt enrich the fictional texture, they are hardly, at this late date, scandalous in and of themselves. No, what is ultimately most shocking about *The Illusionist* is its psychological realism—stark to the point of cruelty—and its unflinching depiction of the heroine's gradual yet complete moral degradation. The book is not simply about a monster (Tamara); it's also about the monster the monster creates (Hélène). True, one is seduced into sympathizing with Hélène at the outset: she seems damaged, friendless, somewhat numb—trapped in a world at once stultifying and emotionally barren. One wonders what she really feels about things—the recent death of her mother, for example, or her respectable father's somewhat clinical turn to Tamara for sexual relief. (The subtle portrait of René—courtly yet passive, comically absorbed in his campaign for local public office—is one of the book's triumphs.) One can see why the Rempart des Béguines—the raffish old bohemian quarter in which Tamara has her flat, exerts such a pull on the heroine. It is a realm of reckless pleasures. That Hélène can also cuckold her own father there—punish him for all his tiresome *bêtises*—only augments the illicit charm.

Yet over the course of the novel the process by which Hélène internalizes the viciousness around her is truly horrifying. Tamara shows the way, of course, and in some of the book's most distasteful scenes—such as the one in which the older woman, eager to assert her power after a quarrel, makes Hélène kneel and beg forgiveness, then proceeds to give her an orgasm in a swift and nasty fashion—might as well be giving her young lover a tutorial in abuse. She's a one-woman mind fuck.

But Hélène is more than a match for her by the end. Indeed, as soon as Hélène learns that Tamara has managed to dupe her father into proposing marriage and is about to become, somewhat farcically, Hélène's new stepmother, she and Tamara—like the strange female couple in Ingmar Bergman's *Persona*—seem to switch places. Tamara's plaintively expressed longing for financial security ("I'm thirty-six, Hélène.... For years I've been wondering whether I'd die in a public hospital or in the street, or simply of hunger in a furnished room") fills the girl with such contempt that not even Tamara's petulant assertion that their affair will continue ("You know that I don't love your father, and that ought to be enough for you") can mitigate the onrushing "feeling of detestation."

She was almost imploring me. I looked at her with disgust. On that face I had loved and admired so desperately, that had been my sun, my horizon, the very incarnation of beauty, cruelty, voluptuousness and suffering, all equally delicious, there was painted that odious humility of beggars and beaten women, that cowardice of irresponsible people, that same weakness that I had hated in myself and that she, unknowingly, had taught me to hate.

Revenge is obviously called for—but what? Telling René about the affair would no doubt put a stop to the wedding and spell disaster for Tamara but, as Hélène recognizes, she too would risk being punished. Her father might well send her to a convent. Then she suddenly apprehends the sadistic power the situation affords her: "If I could not break the marriage, I could at any rate torment Tamara."

It is gambit worthy of Tamara herself. At the novel's end, Hélène is sequestered alone in her bedroom, calmly anticipating the work of emotional blackmail. When she hears her lover rebuffing her father's advances on the staircase outside the room—the wedding has taken place that day and this is the first night Tamara will spend under her new husband's roof—Hélène thinks ("strangely enough") of "those savages who eat the bodies of their ancestors in order, as they say, to inherit their courage. Maybe it did not have much connection with my situation, but that 'No, René,' pronounced in her languorous voice, made me think that perhaps Tamara and I had exchanged personalities." And thus *The Illusionist's* baleful last words: "Alone in the darkness, I began to laugh."

For lesbian readers—especially English-speaking readers—Mallet-Joris's novel may be rough music indeed. True, the book is *hot*—if in a weird, delirious, delicious '50s way. When Tamara's first kiss leaves Hélène "staggering with happiness" it is hard not to appreciate the novelist's voluptuous investment in adolescent ardor. But there is nothing wholesome or redemptive or even coolly amused about Mallet-Joris's view of lesbian love. Nowhere to be found here is any trace of feminist sentiment—any residual notion that Women are Somehow Better. Most of the time they seem Much Worse.

Mallet-Joris once told an interviewer that the plot of *The Illusionist* was based on something that had happened to a schoolfriend of hers. I, too, once had such a "schoolfriend"—one manhandled by a closeted college professor in a manner similar to Tamara's savaging of Hélène. My friend was luckier, though—or else a bit less damaged—than her fictional counterpart. Yet a few years later—just as she was about to begin her own teaching career—she found herself describing to a psychiatrist, once again, the still smarting wound the professor had inflicted. This psychiatrist—a tiny, somewhat cronelike

Swedish woman of immense aura and authority—was silent for what seemed like ages. Then, finally, as if stating the obvious, she remarked, "And now *you* will do the same to someone else." How oddly—my schoolfriend said—the sunlight streamed into the consulting room, illuminating the bizarre plastic pop beads worn by the psychiatrist. My friend made it her subsequent business to disprove the oracle, but even now, almost thirty years later, the struggle to do so still rules her complicated life.

Terry Castle
San Francisco 2006

THE ILLUSIONIST

I

EVERY EVENING AS soon as the stenographers left, the noise of typewriters, telephones, and banging doors stopped, as though a fountain had been abruptly turned off, and once more I was alone in the silence of my third-floor room under the mansard roof, faced with the tedium of my existence. Downstairs in his office, my father had another look at his accounts and the catalogues of his textile firm, took note of the next day's appointments, and consulted the prices on the stock exchange. The last sounds to reach me were the banging of the shutters by André, the half-witted office boy, and the slamming of the door as he finally closed it behind him.

Then it was that I felt my loneliness and wished I could have a chat with someone who took an interest in me. But who was there? My father was too busy to give me even a few minutes of his time. His concern never went beyond casting a glance at my weekly school reports and making an absent-minded comment. "You might do better, Hélène," he would say, when my marks happened to be rather bad. The cook? I dared not dream of it since that day my father had caught me chatting in the kitchen and had said with great finality, "At your age, you shouldn't spend your time with servants!" Yet I would have loved to be down there in the basement rooms where Julia, the cook, often had long and mysterious confabulations with the stenographers. However, they always stopped talking the minute I appeared.

I loved that big, warm kitchen, with its smell of coffee, its copper pans, its blue-and-white curtains. But Julia, so kind in her rough way when we were alone, was different when others were present. She wanted, then, to show off as the unchallenged mistress of these domains. "Hélène, will you kindly go right back up to your room!" she would shout at me whenever I showed up there for a moment, invariably adding, "This is no place for you!" The tone of her voice by no means implied that the kitchen was unworthy of me, but rather that I was trespassing upon a territory forbidden to people of my kind. On these occasions I always returned to my room to sob out my grief and rage. Julia would soon come up to comfort me after her fashion: "Silly girl! Shame on you! Crying about nothing! You're as bad as poor André!" And I would ask, "Then why did you chase me out, Julia?" Whereupon she would take me in her arms and kiss me, upset by my grief but at the same time proud of my affection for her and not knowing how to explain a line of conduct that she herself obeyed without questioning. "What can we do?" she would ask. "My poor Hélène, masters are masters and servants are servants! Society makes these rules . . ."

I was puzzled that this painful distinction not only separated me from Julia and those mysterious conversations but also exposed me to public insult! I was furious with that "society" of stenographers that made my good Julia mistreat me.

But I was not angry with Julia herself. Ever since my mother's death, when I was eight, Julia had taken care of me to the best of her ability. She was a buxom young woman in her thirties, with a fine-featured face, a clear olive complexion, and big black languorous eyes that were always hovering on my father's chauffeur. I was very fond of Julia, for she was the only person in the world who took any interest in me.

The kitchen and my father's office were forbidden regions, but I had free access to the rest of the house: the high-ceilinged dining room with its cordovan leather walls, red damask chairs, and velvet curtains; the stairway landings, with their oak wainscoting and the dark mirrors hanging in the dimly lit staircase; the three drawing rooms, all in a row, crowded with family portraits, heavy sofas and chests, occasional trinkets and ornaments looking as if shriveled up with boredom; the library, with the leaded windowpanes letting in only a subdued bluish light; my mother's room on the second floor, still exactly as she had left it; my father's room, piled high with papers, samples, catalogues; and finally, my own room, at the very top, under the mansard roof. I liked my room because of the view across the plain and because of the tall lime tree reaching up to my window, so near that I could touch its branches with my hand.

I attended Mademoiselle Balde's school, the only "proper" school for young ladies in town, spending a few hours each day there. Decorum was the main thing demanded of the pupils, work was of less importance. I took advantage of this state of things and did nothing.

Sometimes, as I walked home along the steep streets of Gers—the entire town is situated on a hill—I became lost in a dream. I looked at myself in the shop windows as I passed, and saw that I was pretty. I resolved to leave home, go away from this town as soon as I could. I made up childish stories for myself. In one of them, my father and the office workers were all locked up in the big gray stone house and were slowly dying of hunger there, while André, the office boy, auctioned off the furniture. I forgot that I was not yet sixteen, and at times I would be overwhelmed with the desire to run away. It would be better, I thought, to beg by the wayside than to have to go on dying of loneliness! As I walked in the streets I became so lost in reverie, my steps were so weighed down with desires, as well as a feeling of guilt, that I lost all notion of where I was going. It seemed to me that with one step more I might reach the horizon. . . .

Sometimes I would be seen walking along like that, lost in dreams, and Madame Lucette, the bookseller, who lived across the street from us, often called out to me in a worried way when she saw me absent-mindedly going past the door of my house. Then I would quickly speak to her and go into the house, sure she had guessed my wicked thoughts, and as upset as if I had been caught on the street half undressed.

I seldom saw my father. I had no friends. I spoke little, and I read too much, devouring every book I could lay my hands on. Vainly I looked for something worthy of interest and attention in this little town of Gers. And often, bursting into angry tears, I said to myself, "Nothing will ever happen to me in all my life!"

Tall, blue-eyed, strong-faced, his fair hair still without any gray in it, my father, René Noris, was forty-seven years old, wore a beard, and had the strong hands of a working man. He owned several stores, was a successful businessman, and he had a Russian mistress. His square face, usually expressionless, gave a feeling of power. He talked about nothing except business and politics and was given to sudden and brief outbursts of temper which frightened me. At fifteen, this was all I knew about him.

Two years have gone past since then, and I have learned many things which, had I known them then, might have made me think twice. I now realize that my father was very like other men, maybe better than most. Beneath a gruff exterior, he was really weak and kind, and he was sincerely fond of me. But I discovered this too late. It doesn't matter now.

At the time I am writing about, he was so taken up with his work—his stores, his investments, his political ambitions—and with his mistress, whose name was Tamara, that he almost never saw me. Indeed, I seemed to be more of a nuisance in his life than anything else.

He had a hard time finding anything to say to me. "Are you being a good girl?" he would ask. Or, "Do you need anything?" Or, "It seems to me your marks in geography have been rather low, recently." When, as sometimes happened, he had made a mistake, my marks having improved, he would flush and send me away more quickly than usual.

Only once did he take me aside and speak to me at any length. This was when he told me about Tamara.

"Hélène," he said, "you are fifteen years old. You are almost a young lady now, so you can understand—certain things. It's my duty to tell you—to confide in you. I am no different from other men. I—have, ahem . . . There's a young woman in my life, a bond exists between us. I prefer to have you learn this from me rather than hear it suddenly from others. Tamara leads a secluded life. But people are so cruel, so given to gossip . . . They might distort things. Don't think that this fact in my life deprives you of any of my affection. In reality, I'm sure that Tamara herself would . . ."

Suddenly he realized he was going too far and became silent, embarrassed at my impassivity. He dismissed me that day almost roughly.

As a matter of fact, I had not said a word. The revelation left me rather indifferent. I had too few memories of my mother to feel any indignation. But my father had supplied new food for my imagination: Tamara. The name itself was foreign and strange. It gave me, at first, a fleeting and bewildering pleasure, it was like a cold round marble rolling in the hands, a wet flower suddenly crushed. But soon I found something else behind the name Tamara. Madeleine Bégault, a schoolmate of mine, had also heard about Tamara, and once, during a recess, while we were standing under the old pear trees in the paved schoolyard, she even told me she had seen Tamara.

"She has a very bad reputation," said Madeleine. "She lives in the Rempart des Béguines: you know, that dreadful neighborhood near the water front. My mother says the only reason some people have anything to do with her is because your father has lots of money and they know she's his mistress. Just think of it! She's a divorcée!" In her mouth that word acquired an unusual magnitude. Madeleine had once caught a glimpse of Tamara at a party. "But," said Madeleine, "since Mama only told me afterward who she was, I didn't *really* look at her. It seems to me she had short hair, black and curly, and she was wearing a good-looking tailored suit, but I don't remember very well. I understand some people think she's beautiful. But she didn't make much of an impression on me. I don't like tall women, it's so common, it's not fashionable . . ."

She went on talking, but I did not listen.

Now, when my father returned home from his one-night absences, I no longer wondered about the reason for them. I searched his face for a sign of what must have taken place—without exactly stating it to myself I knew it had to do with making love—but he was singularly unromantic-looking and his big bovine eyes seemed to reflect the calm satisfaction of someone who has had a good dinner rather than the exaltation of a happy lover. To console myself, I attributed to Tamara all the poetry my father lacked.

My mind became filled with Tamara. And when Father would induce me to go with him to some reception or other, usually at the house of one of his political friends, I would sit apart on a stool and contemptuously survey all the chattering ladies, bedecked with more feathers than Indian chiefs, or at the young girls in pastel frocks simpering over the cookies and cakes, and I paid no attention to what anyone said. "How different from all these people Tamara must be!" This was my thought, and I longed to know her.

From one reception to another, from dull schoolday to melancholy holiday, time passed, doled out slowly by the church bells which every hour resounded in my snug mansard room, like the roar of waves in a seashell, leaving behind them a murmur of regrets; time passed, in which vague hopes became definite desires, great projects soared only to subside in discouragement. At evening, I leaned out from my window above the rustling garden, gazed at the sky beyond the barren waste of housetops, and whispered to a cloud—for this brief moment sanctified, "Dear God, make me happy!"

At last, when all hope had faded, came the miracle. It did not come as I had childishly imagined it and wished for it. Miracles, when they do occur, disguise their blinding light behind a dull carapace of actuality. The miracle did not come on one of those fateful evenings marked by a crimson sunset or on a poetic night of moonlight. It did not even come during one of those ordinary hours so empty that they seem ready to burst under the sheer weight of emptiness. It came quite simply in the torpor of the after-luncheon hour, slipping in between the half-cleared table, where fruit peelings and the remains of sardines must certainly, you would think, preclude all suspicion of anything unusual; it thrust itself between my father and me, an unwonted and unexplainable presence, but nonetheless perceptible.

"Hélène," said my father, with a strange embarrassment that I sensed, "will you do me a favor? I'm obliged to go uptown, at once. And I had promised . . . I had told Tamara I would see her this afternoon. Will you be so kind as to telephone her to say that, instead, I'll drop in this evening after dinner?"

He did not usually take such a roundabout way to ask me to put through a telephone call for him. I detected in his voice not only an exaggerated sense of decency but also fear—not of me, but of that unknown Tamara. I imagined he was afraid she would be displeased. It was the first time I had ever felt that he was weak, and I was soon to learn that he was terribly weak with her. That day, he *dared not* call her, I realized that immediately. He had plenty of time before leaving, he could have telephoned himself instead of lingering over his newspaper.

"Tell her it has to do with a very, very important customer from Amsterdam who has made an appointment with me. Explain that I did not have a minute to telephone to her myself . . ."

I was surprised at the way he made me his accomplice, his fear having overcome his shame.

"Here's the number. And while I'm about it, I'll give you her address, it's just as well for you to have it, in case something should happen one day, when I am there . . ."

(11)

He scribbled a number and an address on a page of his notebook and handed the paper to me.

"Goodbye, my dear. Don't forget: a very, very important customer . . ."

There was an almost mischievous look in his eye as he rushed away.

For a time I stayed there, sitting stupidly by the fire, behaving like a child that keeps pinching at a balloon, hoping it will burst and at the same time hoping it will not. But provided you don't get tired of it too soon and leave off pinching it, the balloon always ends up by bursting. I was like that with my miracle. I realized I might soon be able to see that envelope of flesh that I had inflated with my dreams. In my still innocent reverie, that "very, very important customer" had just landed like a most obliging dirigible. I had prayed for a miracle—into empty space, it is true, but maybe that was the best way— and now that the miracle was there, it would have been impolite, if not dangerous, to disregard its summons.

But still I did not move. I tried to pretend that nothing much had happened and I remained there, stock-still, in the grip of laziness. The damp wood hissed in the high fireplace that was my father's pride. On the cordovan leather of the walls, lit up by the flames, the gilt parrots seemed to swing in the brown branches. Through the French windows I could see the garden covered with a grayish snow, perforated here and there by a cat's track. It was certainly too cold today to go to the Rempart des Béguines—there was the park to cross. Why go today? Surely there would be other occasions to go there.

But, deep down, what I was feeling was that there existed, on the other side of the park, beyond the frozen lawns, the bare trees, and the nakedness of the statues, a face unknown to me, a face for which I longed as for an unknown land, a face that lived and breathed and was waiting for me, only a ten minutes' run away. Those ten minutes, seen from the dining room, seemed as long as a desert, as unstable as water, as impassable as the film of lucidity separating dream from reality.

No sooner was I outside the house than the wind and the cold gripped me with such violence that without further thought I started to run toward the park. Had it not been for the wind and the cold, I might have turned back; the urge to confront that dream-face with the reality which was waiting there, at the end of my run, seemed less and less urgent. But I continued running to escape the cold. My feet sank into the snow, I was chilled to the bone. Bumping into passers-by, heedless of speeding cars, I reached the park. The paths were dismal. In another hour or so the shop windows, already decorated for Christmas, would light up.

You could feel the approach of the Christmas season in the respectable demeanor of the usual promenaders, their slow, majestic, and paternal gait, their vague smiles. Even the most ossified among them were poking about with their canes, pushing the dead leaves into the hollows of trees, as though making them a cordial gift. I often saw these old men as I crossed the park on my way home from school: they were always the same old people, and I amused myself trying to imagine what their families were like and in what kind of houses they lived. But today I hurried past, intentionally jostling them a little, to bolster up my courage. They turned their heads to stare at me, with empty eyes, like old owls disturbed in solemn council. Then they continued on their way, uncomprehending and resigned.

The cold stiffened my face like a mask and at times I shut my eyes. At last I came out into that narrow and quiet street called the Rempart des Béguines.

In about the year 1900 the building where Tamara lived must have been considered in that neighborhood to be a great work of art, and even now the fishermen and laborers who lived nearby regarded it with perplexed admiration.

The thing about it that first struck you was that every storey had two stone balconies shaped like the prows of ships, jutting out over the street, with gilt chains dangling at either side of them. These balconies were connected, from one storey to another, by caryatids whose heads supported the top balconies while their legs encircled the windows beneath. The composition was really a monstrous jumble: a strange marine temple battered by the waves, since, to give these sculptured females a salty and at the same time decent look, their long, slim, writhing bodies had been veiled with parallel lines and incrusted here and there with shells hiding a too suggestive protuberance. To add to the maritime illusion, whiffs of slimy and fishy odors sometimes invaded the street, for the Rempart was situated not far from the little harbor.

(14)

That building restored my courage. Its unusual aspect fitted in with something I had fantastically and vividly imagined.

I went in. I was not disappointed with what I saw, although the interior must have been "modernized" since the time of the building's construction. Low-ceilinged, dark, with green marble walls, the hall was like a submarine grotto, very comfortably fitted out, for an agreeable warmth prevailed. From behind a dim window glass the concierge peered out with disgusted curiosity at the visitors to the place, as though watching the movements of monsters in an aquarium.

Dizzy and out of breath, I paused a while on the last landing. All was silent. The ceiling was low. There was only one door, of shining mahogany, small and low, like the entrance to a cavern. Beneath a grated peephole was a card in a little silver frame: Tamara Soulerr. Was that name, Soulerr, Russian, or was it the name of the lady's former husband? I had barely time to formulate the thought when suddenly I was in an agony of fear.

This anguished loss of self-confidence was nothing new to me. I was always making great plans and then, just when I had almost realized them, I would feel that fear and lassitude, and would do exactly what I ought not to do, so that the whole project or plan—whatever it was—collapsed. For instance, in drawing class, I would clearly visualize the subject of a water-color painting or a charcoal drawing. I would get everything ready—my paints or pencils—have the dimensions all thought out, and might even set to work. But before having finished it, in sudden exasperation, I would throw down everything and tear up my sketch. Sometimes, too, I'd decide to go down to the harbor, vividly imagining the lime trees, the white yachts ready to leave, the little fishing barks with their brown and orange sails, the lake itself. But I would set out on foot instead of taking the trolley, and before I reached my destination I would be so tired that there was nothing for it but to turn back. Yet I had known in advance that the walk would be too long for me, so why had I set out on foot in the first place? I never could figure it out.

Standing there alone on that landing, I felt I already had enough of poetic mystery. I had seen the house, I had entered it. I could have left quite happily, desiring nothing more for quite a while, but I told myself it would be cowardly to do so. What I was chiefly afraid of was that I might not know what to say to this unknown woman. It was like the fear of not being able to make a good drawing, it was like being afraid the harbor might not really be as lovely as I had imagined it. Mustering all my forces, I conjured up the image of that face, still floating in my dream world like a decapitated flower, and, shutting my eyes, I rang the bell, trying not to hear the rending sound it made on the other side of the mahogany door.

I was weighed down by the silence, and wildly I hoped that no one was at home, that for once I would suffer failure without being responsible for it, but instead, without hypocrisy, could attribute it to an unfriendly fate.

In order the better to hear approaching footsteps, I had practically flattened myself against the door, and when it opened I sprang back in terror.

How long the silence lasted, during which I observed Tamara, I do not know. As though dazzled by the sun, I could not see the face that was at last being revealed to me, but could merely make out the contours. I might have remained for some time in that kind of daze, had not a low voice, rough as a cat's tongue, suddenly brought me back to reality.

"Is there something you want?"

I believe that is what she said, with a little surprise. I did not reply, my throat was too tight, and I was suddenly overwhelmed with despair at the absurdity of this visit. So she added gently:

"Will you come in for a moment?"

There was no entrance hall, so I stepped directly into Tamara's life. Before me was a large, low table, laden with books and covered with the burnt stains left by cigarettes; a big divan upholstered in sailcloth; a phonograph and records beside it on the floor; and, finally, there were shelves crowded with knickknacks which I came to know later on. But upon entering the room only one thing struck me: Tamara's sitting room on the fourth floor did not have one of those prow-balconies, since the large bay window at the end of the room did not overlook the Rempart des Béguines but faced the harbor itself, overlooking several rows of low houses. I could see the entire lake, with a few boats furrowing its yellowish-gray waters.

I had still not said a word, and as I looked around I suddenly caught sight of myself in a mirror. My eyes were like those of a shipwrecked person miraculously cast alive upon a beach, still clasping seaweed in his enfeebled hands. And in truth, though I was not emerging from the ocean depths, I was waking from a dream as alien to this new environment as any ocean depths could be.

Oddly enough, Tamara waited, showing no impatience, as though she guessed that I needed time to get used to this new atmosphere and to find the tone and words suitable for this strange place. I was, however, merely searching for the essential words, knowing I would be able to articulate only a few. The idea of my own voice sounding in this expectant silence frightened me in advance.

"My father . . ." I said. Then, feeling the need of explaining my unwonted presence, I added for no apparent reason, "Please forgive me. My father has been detained in town . . ."

I could not go on, but she had understood.

"You're René's daughter!" she exclaimed, or rather, said, for she did not raise her voice. It was one of her peculiarities which I immediately noted. Never did she raise her voice or change its intensity. She regulated that slightly husky, muffled voice, in which was a trace of foreign accent, with such skill, such delicacy of tone, that she could seem to exclaim, murmur, or speak loudly while the pitch of her voice remained the same and only the inflection changed.

"Ever since your father told me about you, I have wanted so much to meet you," she said. "Sit down. Take off your coat. How nice of René to have sent you! I have been asking him to do this for such a long time. Do sit down! Don't be shy."

Although these pleasant words were said in a drawling

(18)

voice in which I fancied there was some slight irony, my courage revived at the thought that I had been preceded by an introduction. My father had told her about me. My name had already echoed within these dull-blue walls, even my image had perhaps already appeared before Tamara's eyes. Very likely my father had shown her some photographs of me; my face had already become familiar to her.

"He was prevented from coming at the last minute," I said, without any trembling now. "A very very important customer from Amsterdam . . ." I almost smiled as I remembered my father's embarrassment when he had said that.

She did not seem to be unduly interested in the customer from Amsterdam, and I realized how useless had been these precautions. Although, maybe she did not want to show her disappointment in front of me. As a matter of fact, I could scarcely imagine anyone's being disappointed at not seeing my father!

Masterfully, she had led me over to the divan, had taken off my coat, and was now sitting beside me.

"Don't be afraid! I can see you are shy. Very well. You're not obliged to talk, so don't try. I will put the questions and I will answer them myself. I'm used to that. I live alone. If you hadn't come, I'd have been a little disappointed. I was expecting your father to take tea with me. Well, shall you and I have tea together instead? There! I hear the kettle whistling. I'll bring a tray. Only, don't run away while I'm gone!"

Laughingly she stood up. Her laughter did not sound

gay, nor did it sound mundane. It was more like theatrical laughter, both brusk and gentle, pleasant, but strangely out of place. I had started collecting my wits and was now observing her, not without some surprise. I could not say whether she was beautiful or not. Until then I had imagined that beauty was something immutable, predetermined by fixed rules, and I imagined its embodiment in a very white-skinned woman who would be plump—an appetizing morsel, so to speak. This classic beauty would be someone like Madame Lucette of the bookshop. My father had said she was good-looking, with her golden hair done up in a chignon, her fair complexion, her large hazel eyes, and her whole benevolent self, smooth and placid. I also thought that Julia was beautiful, although I felt that only a lack of taste could make me admire her rather angular face with its high cheekbones, her narrow eyes and her olive skin, for no one else seemed to admire her except the chauffeur, who looked at her all day long in blissful rapture.

Tamara—whom people called beautiful—looked more like Julia than Madame Lucette, and I was happy to discover that my judgment of Julia's looks was better than I had thought. Tamara went on talking to me from the kitchen, speaking always in that slow way, with a grain of irony in her tone, as though stressing the unimportance of her words and as though she were talking only to put me at my ease. She returned carrying a tray on which were a teapot, a silver sugar bowl, and two glasses. I was immensely surprised at the glasses, never having seen anyone drink tea out of them. But anyway, tea at three in the afternoon was in itself surprising! I tried not to show my surprise, though.

Tamara bit into a piece of bread.

"I'm not offering you anything else," she said. "I suppose you've had lunch. But I never have lunch, it's such a bore to cook when one lives alone."

She was wearing gray velvet slacks, and a yellow silk blouse, which lent color to her dark complexion. Her cheeks were rather hollow, her eyes were almond-shaped, something like Julia's, her mouth, mauve pink, was pretty. Her short nose was straight and she had the forehead of a stubborn angel, crowned with short curls.

"Now, say something. It's your turn. Say anything, it doesn't matter what, I want to hear your voice."

"Papa did not tell me to *come* here, he only wanted me to *telephone*," I said, without stopping to think.

Again she laughed that strange laugh of hers, which made me uncomfortable.

"You don't talk much, but when you do talk, you say the important thing! What's your name?"

"Hélène."

"How old are you?"

I really could not say "Fifteen and a half." It was such a ridiculous age to be. So I cheated, hoping my father would never contradict me. "Sixteen," I said.

"Sixteen. Why, then, you still go to school?"

"Yes, but not very seriously."

"I imagine your life's none too exciting. You're probably bored. Am I right?"

I have always had a hard time expressing myself, be-

(21)

cause I feel things in a rather mixed-up way and often in two quite contradictory ways. For instance, I was afraid of any change in my life and at the same time I longed for a change that might come about in spite of myself and I believe that if anyone had asked me what I wanted I would have said I wanted everything to remain just the same. I tried to explain all this to this young woman I had never seen before, partly because I wanted to clear up my own ideas and the presence of someone kept me from getting lost in an infinity of details. Also, I had never talked about myself to anyone before, and I was suddenly discovering the charm of confiding in someone. And finally, I wanted to make an impression on Tamara, for I rather groundlessly assumed that people who have led eventful lives must necessarily be superior beings.

She listened to me with profound attention. Later on I was to discover that she showed the same interest in everything that was said in front of her and that she was actually and sincerely interested in what people said to her. I was as if intoxicated: I could have gone on talking forever had I not suddenly remembered—a small detail that seemed catastrophic to me then—that the shirtwaist under my navy-blue uniform had been worn for three days and consequently must be none too clean. I became silent.

She probably attributed this silence to some other reasons, for she touched my cheek caressingly.

"You're regretting having let yourself go!" she said. "Don't be sorry. I was very interested in what you told me. And you'll come again soon. It's not too far away from your house . . ."

It displeased me that she was so sure I would come again. She might have asked my opinion! I hated being treated like a little girl. After all, she wasn't so much older than I, she could not be more than twenty-six or twenty-eight, I thought. This did not give her the right to pat my cheek the way you do a pet animal or a baby, to soothe them. So I replied rather guardedly:

"I shall certainly come again, as soon as I have a moment to spare . . ."

That was the phrase my father always used when he really meant to say: "Never again shall I set foot in this house!"

She looked at me without appearing to be annoyed.

"So, you're not so sure you'll be able to come again, are you? Or of even wanting to? It doesn't matter. You'll see, everything will be quite all right. Now, you must go back home. Let me take that glass that you don't know what to do with! Put on your coat, and run along now."

She seemed to be making fun of me, and anyway I had lost all self-assurance from the minute I had recalled that possibly soiled collar of mine. I had a hard time getting into my coat, I could not find the sleeves, and Tamara just sat there looking at me and smiling, without moving a finger to help me. And what did she mean by "You'll see, everything will be quite all right"? What would be all right? I felt she had been making fun of me all the time.

At the door, my hand on the knob, and ready to escape, I merely said, "Goodbye, Madame."

(23)

"You know very well that my name is Tamara," she said, smiling again. Then she waved her hand slightly, as though to drive me away.

I went out quickly and descended the stairs at a run. I still remember the seagulls that were perched on the balconies.

II

I REMEMBER MY fear. I shall always remember the terror of that week, for it was the first of that kind I had ever experienced. Everything around me had become real, the world had taken on a threatening and concrete reality. An upheaval had occurred in my little girl's world, and the entire landscape had been transformed. I was used to moving in a setting that certainly existed—it would have been too hard to create it out of whole cloth—but a single detail, magnified out of all proportion, had now dwarfed it and reduced it to its pasteboard value.

Formerly I had felt "outside" everything, as though I were looking at other people's lives and at my own life through a glass partition and nothing could touch me. I made an exercise of it. For instance, I would pretend not to know a lesson I had thoroughly learned, and in the midst of the tumultuous classroom, full of murmurs, whisperings, and bursts of laughter, confronting first the surprise then the anger of the teachers, I would sink into a voluntary stupor and not say another word, obstinately fixing my gaze on the desk or the inkwell in order to make this feeling grow in my imagination so that it would occupy all space, so that I could no longer be accessible to anything that went on around me. It had become a routine. In the surroundings of my everyday life I would pick out some ordinary object in which I could become absorbed and hide from the reality of other people. At school it was the red-and-white design of the brick wall; I would spend the entire recess staring, motionless, at it. Or sometimes it would be the black flagstones in the class-room, or, on the opposite wall, the interminable zigzag of the fire escape. In the park it was sometimes the skeletons of leaves; or the interlacing branches of the trees, or the mechanical gait of an old person stiff with rheumatism. In town it was enough for me to evoke the slapping of a sail, the stillness of the little lake, as flat as the palm of your hand, and the screaming of sea gulls rendering the air as palpable as torn cloth. And at home everything—the gargoyle knocker on the front door, my mother's bedroom, where even her comb still lay where she had left it, the little secret stairways, the empty drawing rooms, the library, where I sometimes hid, the stone balcony, from which I would lean with a strange feeling of pleasure—everything was in constant movement before my eyes, everything was alive, at any moment everything frightened me or gave me joy, assumed a benevolent or a hostile look.

But the terror of that week suddenly changed all this and brought it back to human proportions. Without effort and without realizing what I was doing, I had until then been playing with a distorting mirror, and had thereby thwarted all the snares laid for me by the real and logical world. In a single instant Tamara had set everything in order. Perhaps I should have foreseen that my visit to her house would set going an entire mechanism that would henceforth work unfailingly. But to a certain category of innocence nothing is so unpredictable as logic.

Certainly I could have opposed my father's wishes when, without preamble, he announced that Tamara wanted to meet me and that I was to go with him to a reception where she, too, would be an invited guest. I knew my father. I knew he would not force me to accompany him if he thought my objection were dictated by some moral scruple. He even went into explanations on the subject.

"Don't hesitate to tell me if it will be painful to you. I myself am not so keen about it. But this—this person has so insisted . . . I understand it has symbolic value to her, it would be a mark of esteem, or I don't know what! Women are so queer! Will you come along? All you have to do is say something nice to her. You don't have to say much, just a few words. In spite of her—her situation, she is a very fine person, quite worthy of respect . . ."

"Of course I'll go with you, Papa," I replied in a calm voice.

Thinking it over, I was glad Tamara had told him nothing of my visit, and I was curious to know why she wanted to see me again. But as Tuesday drew near, the day I was to meet her at Madame Périer's, I felt a growing discomfort, a kind of apprehension. To be frank, I was afraid.

I used to amuse myself sometimes on the stone balcony

of our house by leaning dangerously over the edge—farther, still farther—until I was almost hanging between life and death. Then I would quickly spring back to safety. With relief I would find myself in the sitting room again, with its clutter of glassware and its changeless odor of dusty velvet. Then, my heart still pounding, I would collapse upon the satin sofa. Well, that day when I agreed to go to Madame Périer's I experienced something of the same kind of fear at the thought of the encounter with Tamara. It was as though, leaning over the abyss, I had for once not managed to spring back to safety.

Tuesday came. Instead of going to school, from where I was supposed to return home to dress, I took a walk in the park, to think things over. The snow had melted. The park was still fresh from the rain that had just fallen. With the greenish dust washed off, the old statues seemed rejuvenated. I walked on amongst these crumbling stones, the fountains where water no longer flowed, the lawns where the hoarfrost was melting, and sat down on the wet bench near the statue of Pomona. My legs doubled up under my wide brown coat, which was as rough and stiff as the bark of a tree, I slowly breathed in the stale odors of winter rain mingled with the smell of pine trees. From the bare branches water dripped upon the yellowish nudity of the marble Pomona. A small tree, fallen, blocked the softened path. I would have liked to be a tree or a stone, so that I might simply enjoy the trees, the sky, and the forest odors. I almost wept as I looked at the perfection of the pale-gray sky, framed in with snow-white clouds. Everything could have been so simple had it not been for all those grownup people! I had forgotten that I was the one that had gone to Tamara's, I was the one who had said nothing to my father about it, and I had forgotten that I had unprotestingly agreed to go to Madame Périer's. Suddenly I felt totally disarmed, innocent, and even persecuted. It seemed to me that my father and Tamara were in league against me to do me an injustice and that, had they not existed, I would have been perfectly happy.

The absurdity of my own reasoning soothed me. Tamara existed, and it was my fault that she existed. It was as childish to wish the contrary as to hope to sink into the earth at a school examination because one cannot find the right answers. Shutting my eyes, I managed for a brief moment to lull all thought by a rhythmic whispering.

A fat and cheerful nurse appeared in the path, dragging after her a flock of toddlers, all muffled up, who began jumping over the fallen tree. The last one fell flat in the mud and howled loudly.

"Bébert!" called the fat nurse. "Hurry up! It's late!"

She gave me an inquiring look as she walked off. Yes, it was late. It was half past three. I must go home and dress for the reception at Madame Périer's. . . .

While I hurriedly changed my clothes and combed my hair I grew calmer. I was no longer positively distressed, but I was still nervous. I still hoped that something—even an accident—would prevent Tamara from putting in an appearance! Even so, I put on my prettiest dress, arranged my hair smoothly in a net, then studied the results in a mirror with some complacency. I looked very much like my father. My eyes, blue green, were like his, and my rather heavy jaw, full lips, and regular features were all inherited from him. It was to my mother that I owed my reddish hair, which, despite its length, was a source of grief to me because of its color.

At last, with my rustling taffeta dress spread out carefully, there I was, beside my father in the car, very conscious of my fine looks, aware of my father's affectionate gaze upon me. He did not know that I had gone to see Tamara without his permission; she had not told him, and that, at any rate, was a good sign.

When we arrived at the Périers', only a few people were in the drawing room, and I saw at once that Tamara was not among them. I was placed in a rather hidden corner, on a taboret behind the large blue sofa where Madame Périer, in a purple dress, sat enthroned. My father moved about the room, shaking hands in a serious way. I, who was familiar with all his expressions, saw that he was already terribly bored. As I looked on, a young man came in. My father, obviously wishing to avoid him, went over to the buffet. But the young man adroitly caught him, held him by the sleeve, and immediately started talking shop. I knew he had only recently gone into business and that what he wanted was to get some tips from my father, whose business reputation was well established. From where I sat I could hear him ask anxiously, "So then, you have faith in cotton?" "Apparently, since I bought some," my father replied drily. "Things are really looking up this year?" the other went on, not consenting to be snubbed. "I had been told that business would be less prosperous this year than last . . ." No doubt my father was cursing his political connections, Madame Périer, and his own weakness in having come; but he was caught, and began to expound his views on cotton.

Meanwhile the tea party was developing along the usual and wished-for lines. Magistrates and industrialists, comfortably ensconced in tapestry armchairs, talked about unjustifiable promotions, arbitrary nominations, and the undeniable corruption of the political campaign. From time to time an argument would spring up between two or three of the guests, but this was rare since, politically, everyone present was in agreement. In one corner, Monsieur Périer, waving his hands like a veritable rug merchant, was holding forth on politics: "When I am asked my profession of faith," said he, "I reply bluntly. In politics it is not permissible to be vague. Not to be frank is to betray one's party. Gentlemen, I will never hesitate to say that I am, in every sense of the word and completely—" he paused, smiled modestly, and went on—"from head to foot, a liberal!"

There was a politely approving murmur. The people there were all friends, or rather, were all in the same boat and were all well bred. But the little barrister was none too popular for all that. He might manage to deliver speeches stamped with loyalist views, but all the same, according to rumor, he definitely leaned to the Left. His pronouncements on communism were well known to everybody. Worse still, he was a bore. I overheard Van Berg, a friend of my father, make a remark in an undertone: "He certainly makes us pay a high price for his stale tea cakes!" My father's back was turned to me, but I heard his whispered comment: "It seems he has some kind of understanding with the Communists." "Which is both stupid and disgraceful!" said the bothersome young man, who hoped to see a revival of the Catholic party.

At that moment, Périer, evidently sensing that he was the subject of conversation, approached my father and spoke to him eagerly.

"Well, my dear Noris! How nice of you to come! I want to compliment you on that speech of yours to the workers. Wonderful to be able to write like that!"

"Oh," said my father, "the one to compliment is my secretary." Outside his business affairs my father was frankness itself and devoid of vanity. "I polish them up, add a few remarks, that's all."

"What you add to the dish is the salt! Without that, it would be tasteless," said the young man graciously, hoping by this flattery to improve cotton quotations on the stock exchange.

My father sighed and moved off with Van Berg. For all the vague political ambitions that he nourished, he did not like salons, and if he frequented them it was because of the service they might render him in his business.

Madame Périer turned toward me.

"My dear, tell me about your studies! Are you going to continue them? You haven't decided? Well, well! At last, a real young lady! You mean to say you don't intend to become either a lawyer, a doctor, an artist, or a social worker?"

"No, Madame."

I was terribly uncomfortable in the midst of all this

loud talk and was still more uncomfortable at having attention drawn to me. So I lowered my head behind the sofa and tried to make people forget me, until I jumped at the sound of a voice not far away.

"*Who* doesn't intend to become a social worker?"

It was Tamara's voice. She had just come in.

Whether because of fear or delight, I am not sure, but I flushed considerably and wished I could sink out of sight behind the sofa, while Madame Périer, who seemed to be at the height of rapture, cried out in a voice that everyone could hear:

"Why, our dear little Hélène, of course! Do you not know her? Well, how amusing! She is the daughter of our friend Noris!"

With this, Madame Périer moved over to make room for Tamara beside her on the blue sofa. Her object was, doubtless, less to compliment Tamara than to bring us together. This, she thought, might prove to be interesting! I also believe she imagined our meeting to be accidental and that my father would be displeased. But he remained at the other end of the drawing room, having greeted Tamara with a smile, and did not seem to be at all put out of countenance.

As for Tamara, she held out her brown hand over the back of the sofa in the simplest possible way. Disappointed, Madame Périer turned aside, and the conversation once more became general. The ladies there also talked politics, after their own manner, but with assurance. Whereas hats took only a few months to reach Gers from Paris, fashionable ideas, on the other hand, were

(33)

renewed only every few years. These ladies were all audaciously feminist, they discussed free love, adultery, and woman's rights fiercely, calling a spade a spade. This did not prevent them from heartlessly dismissing a maid who "misbehaved" or an unfortunate kitchen girl who managed to get pregnant by the milkman on his daily rounds.

I did not listen to the conversation but centered all my interest on Tamara. She was wearing a light-gray tailored suit, very inconspicuous but, it seemed to me, elegant, with the same yellow silk blouse that I had already seen. I had been thinking so much about her that the uncertainty in which I still was as to whether or not she was beautiful suddenly vanished. I already loved her face, with its slightly hard lines, its crown of black hair, in which almost blue lights showed, the flexible line of her brown neck as she bent forward or sat up in front of me there on the sofa. No one was now looking at me. I could observe Tamara in comfort. She was "making conversation," was smiling coquettishly at some important men, according special deference to men in the legal profession, replying at exactly the right moment to a young married woman who was being rather aggressive. Her voice was as usual calm and had that hint of irony in it.

"How interesting," she said, "to have a part in all these matters! I suppose your husband always asks your advice? He most certainly should, for there are so many things that only a woman's sensitive mind can understand . . ."

I wanted to hug her, for there was no doubt that she was making fun of the pretentious young woman, whom I detested.

"Oh, of course, I try to do what I can," simpered this person. "But it's my principle never to lend aid to the collaborators in the recent war. For instance, not long ago my husband let me read a letter from a prisoner. If one were to believe that letter, the writer was a poor devil who had been denounced and calumniated by jealous neighbors. I told my husband, who is always too good-hearted, 'If I were in your place, Jacques, I'd go ahead with my investigations . . .' "

Tamara listened, with rather weary signs of approval. But—and only I could see this—her strong brown hand, which was hanging over the back of the sofa, was impatiently scratching the silk.

I was submerged in a wave of tenderness, so sudden that tears came to my eyes almost simultaneously. I had never had a friend, I had never had anyone to whom I could describe how I loathed and detested the people of Gers, or to whom I could speak of my childish desires for adventure and describe my strange daydreams. I had even thought that I would never find anyone in Gers who could understand me. I had thought that only mean and stupid people like Madame Périer lived there, or else rather obtuse people like Julia or hypocrites like my father, who was as bored as I was by all these social gatherings but fiercely refused to admit it. And suddenly I had discovered someone who was interested in me, and who surely shared my contempt for this "society" devoid of interest. It was someone whom my father would not prevent me from seeing and whose own life must be wonderful. I could not get over the thought that a person so perfect actually lived in Gers and also happened to live in the most picturesque neighborhood and in the strangest house—a house where I could go, from now on, as much as I liked. I sighed with happiness.

My agony of fear had completely vanished. I could not even understand why I had been afraid. Sitting there out of sight, on my taboret between the wall and the sofa, I experienced the same happiness I had often had in the library, sitting between the roaring stove and the shelves full of books, but with a greater intensity. I suddenly felt *good*. I loved my father, I wanted to be first in my class, I resolved to keep my exercise books in impeccable order, I resolved all sorts of things: to work harder, to say my prayers every night, to rake the garden as my father liked me to do, and to remember to put crumbs out on the roof every day for the sparrows. . . .

It was a gray day outside. Within doors they had had to light the lamps, and in their dim rosy glow Tamara's face was still more beautiful. Those two bitter lines at her mouth had disappeared, her forehead was smooth, and now her smile looked almost gentle. Oh, it was a marvelous thing to be sitting there in that salon where so often before I had been bored to death, surrounded by the faces of the same people who had formerly got on my nerves, but to sit there, now, in the shadow of such beauty!

Her hand still lay on the back of the sofa. I noted that she wore a silver signet ring with the initial "E" on it. From time to time she turned round toward me, and the others must have thought she was talking to me. But she did not say anything, she just looked at me out of the corners of her eyes, and I was unable to make out exactly the meaning of that look, for there was in it both mockery and affection, and she seemed to be commanding something of me. Yes, she was asking something of me, I seemed to understand it better than if she had spoken. I struggled against my impulse for several minutes. I felt cold, my temples throbbed. I was afraid I might fall off my taboret in front of all these people who would have laughed. At last I resisted no longer, but bent forward quickly, as if to pick up something, and pressed my lips against the hand of Tamara.

The ladies of Gers, all these wives of magistrates and officers, who think they simply must kiss young girls on the cheeks—wet kisses through veils—are usually not perfumed or, if they are, it is always with violet or lavender, or maybe with Chypre—supreme extravagance. Well, Tamara's hand smelled of Eau de Cologne, leather, and tobacco. Again I had an almost pleasant sensation of dizziness.

My father came up, looking for me.

"Oh, there you are! It's time to go. Hurry, my child. I must stop off at the stockrooms before seven o'clock, and two people may already be waiting for me at the house."

I plucked up my courage.

"Couldn't I stay a little longer, Papa?"

"Yes," Tamara gently interposed, looking him straight in the eyes. "Couldn't you let her stay on a few minutes? I can see that she gets home! I've so enjoyed making her acquaintance . . ."

Apparently Papa had no desire to enter into an argument in public, for he immediately consented.

"Very good," he said lightly. "I'll send the car back for you both in a quarter of an hour. Goodbye, my dear."

I did not recover my wits until he had gone through the door.

"Come, sit here, pretty child," Madame Périer murmured, making room for me between herself and Tamara.

I thought I was dreaming. And as though in a dream I came forward with a miraculous ease, without bumping into anyone, without even touching the table that was dangerously loaded down with cups and flowers. While replying as best I could to questions asked me, I forced myself to note all the little concrete details of my surroundings, to prove to myself that I was really in the salon of that Egeria of liberalism, Madame Périer. There was the table, the half-emptied teacups, the dried-out sandwiches, and the slightly stale cakes. I looked at them, but I did not really see them. I had trained my imagination too well to concentrate on one single object, and so, I could not see or hear anything or anybody but Tamara. Everything else seemed to float in a miraculous fog.

"The car must be waiting for us now," Tamara said to me suddenly. "Shall we go down and see?" Then, to Madame Périer, "May I say goodbye, dear Madame?"

"Why yes, of course," replied the latter venomously. "Do take advantage of the Noris car while you can!"

While Tamara was bidding goodbye to some other people, I slipped out quickly and waited for her on the landing, pretending to look at the drawings that were hung there—various landscapes and one large charcoal drawing of a nude woman. Tamara came out of the salon and closed the door behind her.

"Let's wait a minute here," she said. "I don't think the car has come yet, but I couldn't stand it any longer. Oh, how I detest those people! Did you ever hear of such a thing, to have a reception in a room where the family portraits are draped in crepe! It was like being at a funeral!"

There had indeed been three family portraits on the drawing room wall that were surrounded with a black band. I gave a nervous laugh, which I quickly stifled.

We were alone on the dark landing, with the silent stairway before us. Below, in the vestibule, glimmered a wrought-iron lantern. You could hear the confused murmur of the guests in the drawing room, and from time to time a gust of wind rattled the windows. What were we doing, standing there in the semi-darkness, not daring to raise our voices?

"It's going to snow, soon," I said in a trembling voice. I no longer felt like laughing. Tamara smiled, without replying, and I could see her just well enough to read the look on her face, which again wore that complex expression in which a strange tenderness was mingled with irony.

It was exactly at that moment that I again felt that fear of mine. I well realized that there was something frightening in the attraction I felt for Tamara, something resembling the desire I had to plunge into empty space, when I leaned out of the window, something like what I felt when

I swam toward the dangerous eddy in the lake—"just to see . . ."

A phrase kept running through my head, confusedly, like a fugitive glimmer of light, like a dancing firefly. It was absurd of me, I was ashamed of it, but I couldn't help repeating it over and over without even understanding or realizing for a second what it meant: *"Et Phèdre au labyrinthe avec toi descendue, se serait avec toi retrouvée ou perdue"*—"And Phèdre would have gone down into the labyrinth with thee, and with thee would have been either rescued or lost . . ."

One of my favorite games was to repeat a verse until I had forgotten everything but its cadence. I often amused myself doing that, and sometimes I went so far as to lose consciousness of all else. But now I was repeating the phrase against my will, for what I wanted now, with all my might, was to reflect, to comprehend what was happening before it was too late, as I stood there on that dark landing saying nothing, breathing with difficulty, and listening to my own breathing. My imagination carried me off against my will, and I seemed to be watching something from a great distance, without understanding or caring about what was happening, while my own voice whispered the line from *Phèdre*. I had misquoted it at first. Phèdre did not use the intimate form of address with Hippolyte. Nor did I with Tamara. The line was, correctly: *"Et Phèdre au labyrinthe avec vous descendue, se serait avec vous . . ."* With *you*, not with *thee*. Why had I misquoted it the first time? And why was I thinking of that verse at all? Oh yes, it was because of the word *perdue*.

Lost. I was thinking: "*Hélène au labyrinthe avec toi descendue, se serait avec toi retrouvée ou perdue. . . .*" How Tamara would have laughed had I suddenly told her what I was thinking about, what I was whispering there in the semidarkness. Or maybe she would not have laughed. Maybe she would have understood. Understood what? Something I did not understand myself?

It seemed as though I had become two people, or as if a part of myself remained there, motionless, holding hard to that strong and comforting hand. Had I taken her hand? Or had she taken mine? And another part of me, very far away, was trying to see and understand what was happening, distracted by that inner voice which kept on saying over and over again: "*Et Phèdre au labyrinthe . . . Et Phèdre au labyrinthe . . .*" Always ending on the final word, *perdue*. Lost. Lost . . .

A violent ringing of the doorbell brought me back to myself. For a minute I looked round me, frightened as if out of a dream. For how long had we been there without saying anything? What had Tamara been thinking? Had someone come out of the salon, I would not even have been aware of it!

She led me to the stairs as if I had been blind. The car had just arrived. I got in first, letting myself sink down upon the cushions with as much aching weariness as if I had taken a long walk. And, without thinking about what I was doing, I laid my suffering head on a shoulder that was waiting for it. . . .

Through the car window I saw the dismal streets slip slowly past, I saw the little shops huddled behind their awnings, the trolley cars clanking along slowly, carrying people who looked benumbed with cold, and conductors with red noses. We soon reached the park and speeded across it beneath the trees. The empty benches glistened with patches of frost. At the corner of the Rempart des Béguines, a policeman, powdered with snow, was warming himself by jumping up and down, first on one foot, then on the other.

"And here we are!" said Tamara as the car approached her house. "It was a nice afternoon in spite of all the society stuff. I was so glad to see you. Until Thursday, then."

"Thursday?"

"Why, yes, Thursday. Toward three or four o'clock if you like. I'm not free tomorrow afternoon."

"Yes," I said. I would have been incapable of saying anything else. Without the shoulder to rest upon, I was trembling again; the delightful anguish affected my knees. If I had been able to describe the feeling I had, I would have used the word "terrible." A terrible sweetness. That was it.

The car had stopped in front of her house. The façade was rendered even more weird in the evening light. Only the gilded chains of the balconies still shone with what remained of daylight. Tamara opened the car door and as she got out she pressed her cool lips upon my cheek.

Through the rear glass I watched her disappear into her maritime temple, watched the Rempart des Béguines recede out of sight. It was dark, and snow was falling.

III

ALL THAT I know about Tamara I learned a little at a time, putting together what scraps of information I could find in old letters, a photograph album, and remarks she occasionally let fall. She had little liking for intimate talks about herself. For one thing, she detested failure, and it seemed to her that she had not made a success of her life. She was a strange mixture of hurt pride and frustrated ambitions that were still sufficiently alive, and she combined with a fundamental indifference a passionate interest in human beings. All this was mixed up with other things that still puzzle me, even today, but which often made her act incoherently. At least, that is how I explain, at present, her strange self-assurance, her efforts to meet me, and the almost impatient way she received me when I rang her doorbell, as she had asked me to do, on the following Thursday.

She came to the door in a dressing-gown, her curls in a tangle over her smooth forehead, looking sleepy and irritated. Before letting me in, she stared at me for a moment, as though she did not recognize me.

"Oh, it's you!" she said, at last. "I was asleep."

For an instant I thought she was going to send me away. As I went into the big blue room I cast a bewildered glance at the disorder that reigned there. The two leather armchairs were overturned, the table was littered with cigarette stubs, as on the day of my first visit. Tamara stamped out her cigarettes just anyhow and anywhere, never swept up except once a week, and books and phonograph records littered the floor. That day, in spite of my confusion, I was able to look at the knickknacks on the shelves, at the glass objects and African masks. At the end of the room a white kitchen showed through an open door.

I expected Tamara would at least make some explanation of this incredible disorder, but she did not. My father had brought me up—if, indeed, one may say that I had been given any kind of upbringing—to think of order as one of the qualities essential to a human being, and to believe that to lack it was to lack the most elementary sense of one's own dignity. Judging from this topsy-turvy room, must I conclude that, on this point as on others, he had made statements that belied his thoughts? Or was it that his passion for Tamara was so great that he bore with resignation such a state of things?

I imagined that Tamara made an effort, before his visits, to do some tidying up in the room—and I was not entirely mistaken. Later on I realized that my father, without any hypocrisy whatsoever, could detest disorder at home and almost suffer physically from it, while rather liking to encounter it elsewhere, and in this case he considered it picturesque, a setting that added to his feeling of being in quite another element when with Tamara. It was attractive in the same way that this strange house was attractive, for it amused him as much as it did me. The house was amusing; but he would not have wanted to live in it for anything in the world. When I understood this, I realized also that he was not as devoid of imagination as, with my little girl's vanity, I had once and for all decided he was. But his imagination was for him only a kind of diversion, an agreeable relaxation, while I, by repeated exercises and without noting it clearly, had made of my imagination a monster that devoured everything, even my will power.

While I was thinking some of these thoughts, Tamara freshened up her face with some Eau de Cologne, then combed her thick curls in an absent-minded way, paying no more attention to me than if I had not existed.

"The apartment is inconvenient," she said at last in a flat voice. "It's just a succession of rooms, badly arranged, all along the back of the house."

She went into the kitchen, and I thought it was the thing to do to follow her. I had imagined without any further thought, having had a glimpse of the kitchen, that her apartment consisted only of that big room into which one entered suddenly. But I found out now that the kitchen led into another room, which served Tamara as bedroom.

The bedclothes were turned down and it was obvious she had got out of bed to open the door. Beside the bed, a full ashtray was placed directly on the floor, near an open book. The parquet shone. The absence of rugs in this apartment agreeably surprised me. At home I detested the way people could suddenly appear without warning because of the thick carpets that muffled the least sound. The window, as big as the one in the other room, also overlooked the lake. This bedroom was even more empty than the other room. The only pieces of furniture, besides the bed, were an inlaid chest of drawers and a leather armchair.

Tamara threw her Persian dressing-gown on the armchair. She was wearing pale-blue pajamas and leather slippers. I admired her slim figure and I thought her costume very elegant, mentally comparing it with the nightdresses I wore, baggy old things with nosegays on them. Julia made them for me, one after another, as they wore out, and they were always exactly alike.

"It's a lovely view," she said, "but sometimes I hear the music in the cafés all night long."

"Oh, and that keeps you from sleeping?" I asked politely, dimly aware that there was something absurd in the stiff way I was addressing her, I who loathed the manners of the "well-bred young ladies" with whom I was compelled to associate. But she had not encouraged me to speak to her in any other way.

She had sat down on the bed. Now she cast off her leather slippers and stretched herself out between the sheets. I felt perfectly ridiculous standing there in front of her, encumbered with my coat and brief case—I had just come from school—and I flushed with anger. She had practically ordered me to come, yet there I stood as though unwanted, and I felt she was enjoying my embarrassment. My line of conduct was clearly laid down for me: I ought to leave, go back home, disregard her remonstrances. Ah, but I was not at all sure she would remonstrate, and, oddly enough, that was what checked me. At last she spoke.

"Put down your brief case against the wall," she said calmly, as if I had just arrived. "And take off your coat. Put it on the chair. That's right. Now, come and sit down here beside me."

When I was seated on the bed she surveyed me, with an expression on her face that I had not yet seen there—almost kindly.

"You're going to have to decide right now, darling, that you won't hold any grudge against me," she said, and I was struck by the intimate tone she adopted, as if out of long habit. "I'm not always gay. And I have many reasons not to be. Don't pay any attention, it's not important and you can't do anything about it. Simply take things as they come and don't worry yourself about anything."

I was astounded at the way she spoke; you would have thought it had been decided straightaway that I was going to spend the rest of my life with her.

"Tell me what you were thinking about last night," she said gently.

Despite her disconcerting attitude I felt I could trust her. And so I tried to explain everything: how I sometimes felt I was two people, or rather, that a part of me vanished out of sight sometimes, and about the line from *Phèdre* that haunted me, that line in which Phèdre wishes she and Hippolyte might have gone down into the labyrinth together: *"Et Phèdre, au labyrinthe avec vous descendue . . ."*

(47)

She interrupted me after a few minutes.

"Dear child! You're too imaginative—far too imaginative!"

"I'm not such a child," I protested, "and you're not so old, either."

"I'm thirty-five years old."

"Oh!" I exclaimed, and could think of nothing else to say in reply to that surprising statement. But upon observing her more closely, I noted the slight lines at the corners of her eyes, the hollows in her oval cheeks, the dark rings which, that day, encircled her eyes, and no caress could have moved me more than did these signs of fading beauty.

"Thirty-five years. To you that doesn't mean a thing. But to me it means a lot. It means all the things I have let slip through my fingers: a marriage, a fortune, a true love. Thirty-five. And I'm still not resigned, not quite. Here I am, my dear, stuck in this small town! Well, after all, I started out in a small town, as small as Gers, even smaller. And I lived in a shanty there, worse even than this old call-house where I live now. . . ."

I was on the point of interrupting her to say I liked this house very much and also to ask her what a call-house was. But I contained myself, fearing a rebuff of some kind, afraid she would stop talking. She was looking at me affectionately—or so I thought.

"You, too, will go out into the world from a small town. For you do dream of leaving this place, don't you? I wonder where you'll end up! I can't give you advice. I've always known what I should have done myself, but I've never done it. Maybe things will be easier for you, you're so innocent. . . ."

Her frankness touched me to the quick. I foresaw a long friendship, with thrillingly intimate talks. It seemed to me I had at last found a refuge, a place away from home where I would be welcome whenever I liked. For a second time I kissed her hand.

She surveyed me with curiosity.

"Take off your shoes, darling," she said softly, as if it were the most natural thing in the world.

It took me a terribly long time to untie my shoes. My hands were trembling so much that I had to start over again several times. At last it was done.

"And your skirt . . . and your blouse. . . . That's right. Now, come to bed."

I was trembling uncontrollably as I got into bed. My hairnet came undone, and I heard her voice—I dared not look at her—saying in a perfectly calm and normal way, "You have beautiful hair."

Instinctively I sought her shoulder to hide my face there; I felt that something frightful was about to happen. But, tilting up my chin, she forced me to look at her.

"Surely," she asked, "you're not afraid? Not really! At your age?"

She had raised herself a little, propping her elbow on the pillow, and I was lying stiffly, very ill at ease and overwhelmed with terror. But then she leaned out from the bed and apparently turned the dial of a radio placed on the floor, for soon soft music could be heard.

"There! That's better, isn't it?" she said, drawing my head down upon her breast. "Don't say anything. Just relax."

I obeyed. Soon I could listen to the music with greater

ease of mind. My faculties returned and I began to wonder what I was doing there, half dressed, in this lady's bed.

I was particularly upset at the thought of my underwear. Out of a spirit of contradiction, and so as to be different from my schoolmates, who only thought of laces, embroideries, and silks, I affected underwear of coarse, unbleached linen. But that day I would have given anything to be wearing the kind of lingerie I so despised. However, I stared at the ceiling, with its false beams, and gradually I felt better. Tamara's hand was smoothing my hair.

"A little heartened, now, darling? You aren't cold, are you?"

I shook my head.

"Still not ready to talk, I see. But make an effort! Talk to me about yourself, like you did the other day."

I tried, but could not utter a word.

"Say something—no matter what!"

She seemed to be slightly out of patience, which paralyzed me still more. Again she tilted up my face and seriously studied me.

"Listen, my child. If you haven't said something within five minutes, I'm going to slap you! Say something, if only 'Oh!' Come now, take your choice."

She did not seem to be in the least angry, but I realized this was no mere threat.

"I'm afraid!" I whispered, almost involuntarily.

"That will do for a beginning," she replied with great calm.

But the shock I had sustained at her threat, added to

my fear and embarrassment, made me burst into tears. At once she drew near me and took me in her arms. I felt her lean, well-muscled body next to me: it was like a boy's. She put one arm beneath me, cradling me, and my tears flooded her neck and breast.

I have always liked to cry, and at fifteen I cried over anything: a book, a dog run over in the street, a hard word, a beautiful landscape, even, a concert, a melancholy song, and it was as though my heart were torn apart, breaking in my breast, with a delightful pain. Julia had often taken me like that in her arms and her soothing words had always brought me a confused but immediate pleasure. So, in the arms of Tamara, I tasted that joy of being consoled and embraced, of hearing the murmur of tender words, and it seemed to me that this pleasure had its natural sequel in the long kiss that followed. . . .

I had never kissed anyone like that before and, though I had listened to my schoolmates chattering about a shameless girl who allowed herself to be kissed on the mouth by all the boys at the *lycée*, I had had no idea of what a kiss was like. Indeed, for several weeks following this first kiss, I was under the delusion that it was Tamara's own marvelous invention. Then, one day, I decided to satisfy my curiosity and I looked closely at some lovers kissing in the park, a thing I had always avoided doing, out of a kind of disgust, and I was disillusioned.

So then, that kiss was for me a total and marvelous revelation. She had barely stopped kissing me when I again held up my lips to hers, and that accord between us was at once perfect. Later on she completely undressed me and fondled me lightly with her hand, almost as one pats a horse; but I could think of nothing else. The pleasure of kissing her seemed to me complete enough, and I could not get over the delightful confusion of being so close, like that, to another person, a thing I had never imagined possible. And between her kisses, of which I could never weary, I told her everything, pouring out a jumble of confessions, telling her everything I had ever dreamed, imagined, or desired. I even made up some things, when I saw that she was interested, and I fairly jumped when she said, with calm authority, "Now it's time for you to dress, darling, and go home."

I was staggering with happiness as I left her, and I touched caressingly the walls, the trees, the snow. It was two days before Christmas and I felt that I had received a gift from heaven.

So that was the way it all began between Tamara and me.

IV

At first sight, comparing me with her portrait, you might say I look like Emily. Even I thought so, when I found that big photograph in Tamara's album. It gave me a kind of shock. But when I looked at it more closely, I soon discovered how superficial this resemblance was. Emily had light-brown hair, big eyes, regular features—like me. But you quickly saw that her expression was colder and, I must say, more intelligent. According to Tamara, I have a bovine look in my eyes. I consoled myself when Tamara said this by applying to myself the complimentary Greek epithet "ox-eyed."

Emily's features were also finer and more forceful than mine. From all accounts, she must have been very different from me, and I could not at all hope to be a rival of this girl, who had been the great love of Tamara's life.

I learned much less about her from Tamara (it always hurt her to talk about Emily) than from reading the old letters Tamara had kept and which, with her usual negligence, she let lie about in the unlocked drawers of her dressing table. You could see at once that Emily's hand-writing was the exact opposite of mine. It was big, firm, angular, with the bars of the *T*'s and *F*'s neatly drawn. It showed decision and obstinacy. While mine, oh heavens, was the writing of a schoolgirl; it showed effort, the letters were round and slightly shaky; it was just the kind of writing for ruled exercise books where you would expect to see the note: "Good work, but a little too stiff and academic." I suffered over my writing as much as I did over my face, for though you might manage to think that my face looked like a German madonna's, it seemed to me that it lacked character terribly. There was something keen and demoniacal in Emily's face, while mine, when not upset by some strong emotion, reflected a complete serenity.

As a matter of fact, I never saw Emily. But I was obsessed with her existence for several months, so it seems to me I ought to tell a little about her and about Tamara before I came into Tamara's life.

Tamara had left her native village in Russia and her poverty there to go to Paris as the bride of an Armenian Jew, Ezra Soulerr, who had happened to be attracted to her. She was then sixteen, could neither read nor write, and spoke only a dialect that even real Russians barely managed to understand. She was dazzlingly beautiful at that time, and the merchant was delighted with her ignorance and wildness. He had practically bought her when he married her, and so he thought he had bound her to him for life. But after five years in Paris she could read, write, and speak French perfectly and from then on was quite able to amuse herself without him, go out alone, and choose her own clothes.

Soulerr was as proud of her as if she had been his own creation. Never did he introduce her to his friends without bragging about how he had improved her, as if she were a trained animal. Very soon this pompous attitude offended her, for she had become aware that he was fifty years old, thin and bald, and that, though he was a man of intelligence, he was destructively so. In society he behaved pleasantly enough, but he despised everyone; he liked to render services, but did so out of sadism, for it pleased him to have people he despised need him, justifying his contempt for them by their servility. He professed that this was a characteristic of his race, but even such cynicism annoyed Tamara. Happily, she had also discovered that he was a rich man and, thanks to his generosity, she was able to put his wealth to some use. So it was that she acquired for herself a big apartment, furnished it luxuriously but in sober taste, and bought a car and a saddle horse.

Soulerr observed her with amused curiosity, letting her do absolutely as she liked. He had expected her to display barbarous taste and throw herself upon jewels, laces, and elaborate costumes. Instead, she affected tailored suits or, when at home, slacks, refused to show off her beautiful shoulders in evening gowns, and her apartment reflected the same willful sobriety and force. Soulerr smiled to himself when he saw her stride into her room in riding breeches and throw her thick gloves or riding crop upon a low table; her masculine affectations amused him. He loved her room, which he laughingly called "the stable" or "the garage," but feeling that her desire for independence was unconsciously directed against him, he took a sly delight in destroying, by his very presence, any illusion of freedom in Tamara's mind. Little by little he accustomed himself to take most of his meals and his amusements in the company of Tamara's most recent female adorer and noted how Tamara treated all her women friends with a high hand, out of an unconscious feeling of vengefulness. He told himself that all these inclinations of Tamara were more reassuring than anything. So he restricted himself to reminding her of his presence from time to time with a stinging word, which made her grow pale with fury. He told himself that it was amusing to tame her like that; he did not realize that he loved her.

He had accorded Emily the same reception as the other women friends of his wife, a little surprised at her youth —she was not yet twenty—and the strange freedom allowed her by her parents. She had come from the Isle of Jersey to Paris to learn French, and would remain two years. Her fine, expressive face rather pleased Soulerr. He considered her of no importance. When, therefore, Tamara left him to go and live with Emily, his amazement knew no bounds. Nonetheless, he continued to give Tamara a small allowance, pretending to do so out of sheer nobility, but in reality in the hope of winning her back some day.

She set up housekeeping with Emily in a small, sunny apartment, almost monastically furnished, where the young girl went on with her studies. The amount Soulerr gave Tamara had been carefully calculated: it was just enough to keep her from working—he knew all too well that she was too improvident to work unless literally driven to it by dire need—and just enough to oblige her all the same to ask for an advance each month. Every time she came to his office for this money, he counted it out slowly, watching her face, trying to detect a fugitive blush, a droop of the eyelid which would show her bitterness or regret. But Tamara's expression, as she looked at the inlaid furniture, the paintings, and the silver ash trays, showed merely cheerful acceptance. "One can't have everything," it seemed to say.

I know very little about her affair with Emily, except that it lasted for two and a half years, that it was passionate and tempestuous, but happy, altogether. I read the letters Emily wrote to Tamara once when they were separated for the summer. They made me blush. Finally, Emily left her to go away with a "fine young man," a Belgian engineer who was going to the Congo. I know even less about the period that followed this great grief in Tamara's life and which preceded our encounter. From stray remarks of hers it seems to have been a period of furnished rooms, cheap restaurants, and third-class railway tickets. I had to guess at all the hidden events in that period of apathetic misery, dunning creditors, ill-tempered concierges, clothes that had to be pawned or sold, brief but necessary love affairs.

What had made her come to Gers? How had she met Max Villar, the artist who, out of pity, had provided her with this apartment in the Rempart des Béguines? These questions remained unanswered. When I met her, she had been living in this apartment for two years, during which time my father kept her in a small way. Between his visits she filled in her time with the books that she fairly devoured, the tea and cigarettes with which she intoxicated herself—these were no doubt the cause of most of her moodiness—and occasionally she would indulge in a whole bottle of whisky.

The second time I went to see Tamara she did something more than kiss me, and what she taught me worried me a little for quite a while afterward.

Once, very vaguely, one of the teachers at school had talked to me about bad habits that destroy our health and produce terrible maladies. I had not paid much attention at the time to what she said. (But I now think that she attributed my continual absent-mindedness and apathy to things of this sort.) After I understood what these "bad habits" were, I became a prey to anxieties that were all the greater for being nebulous. Even the pleasure I took in these caresses seemed to me an indication of sickness, and without daring to talk about it to Tamara (more than anything, I was afraid of her mockery) I worried myself almost to death without knowing what to do.

As to moral scruples, I had none. On the first day, as I sat down at table, I had trembled lest my father, unexpectedly endowed with powers of divination, might read on my face what had transpired, and in class I was afraid that someone might suddenly point a finger of shame at me, my countenance having betrayed me. But very quickly I realized that no one saw anything. Indeed, on the contrary, people began to congratulate me on not being so often lost in dream, and on listening more attentively to what was said to me. Triumph of immorality! My marks in class—and this was what embarrassed me—noticeably improved. Formerly deplorably low, they rose to such an extent that it could be foreseen that this year, for the first time, I would not be obliged to repeat my examinations.

Finally, an imprudent step on my part contributed to dissipate my last fears. My father had a childhood friend, Frédéric Van Berg, who enjoyed an execrable reputation throughout the town. Without anyone's being able to prove a thing, it was said that he had been the lover of many ladies of the best society of Gers, that he had seduced some young girls, and that he was often seen in the cabarets of Versaint, the "big town" nearby. I supposed that this dissolute man would doubtless condone my misconduct and reflected that no one could better inform me as to the dangers I feared from it. I therefore went to see him at his office. Like my father, Frédéric Van Berg was an industrialist. But having inherited a rather big fortune, he worked less hard and chiefly occupied himself with affairs on the stock exchange. All the same, every day he was punctiliously at his office in our neighborhood from three to five—some people said he kept a bachelor establishment there as well.

To go to see him like that was to take an insane risk. The fact that Frédéric Van Berg was my father's friend should have kept me from even thinking of such a thing. However, I was not disappointed in him. He took it all as a joke, seemed to be amused at what I told him, and finally reassured me. He did not even have to promise me that he would say nothing about it to my father. He acted like an accomplice, and the very fact that Tamara was my father's mistress seemed to add spice to this curious adventure, as far as he was concerned. For my part, I confess I had never even thought about that phase of it. The idea that my father enjoyed similar moments of intimacy with Tamara never crossed my mind, did not ever bother me, strange as that may seem. Partly because his time was limited and partly out of natural courtesy, he never visited her without warning her in advance by telephone, and rarely did his visits surpass the rhythm of once or twice a week—"Simply for hygienic reasons," said Tamara, who never seemed to look forward to them with any eagerness. She made preparations for them, nevertheless, by clearing away the cigarette stubs and by stuffing away in her chest of drawers everything that littered the floor, then locking it up. Tidied up in this way, the apartment kept its bohemian look, while being neat and clean. But never did these preparations awake in me any other thought than that of Tamara attending to a tedious job.

Van Berg dismissed me with a pinch on the cheek, and gaily proposed that I come see him, if ever I wearied of the pleasures dispensed by Tamara. He said he would know how to make me appreciate other kinds of pleasures!

I felt much easier as I left him, and from that time on I organized my whole life round the Rempart des Béguines.

The winter went by peacefully. Near my window the branches of the lime tree rattled in the gusts of wind. The cat remained crouching near the fireplace, the children went sliding in the street, the fishing barks no longer left the harbor but let their sails hang useless. It was always dark when I reached home, but I no longer feared bad characters hidden amongst the bushes as I crossed the park. I felt I was now a completely grownup person.

I had given up indulging in "poesy," as I called it, those continual games of my imagination and that deformation of life which had been on the point of becoming second nature. I believed—although I had not yet read Rimbaud, I used the term that I was later on to find in his writings, much to my naïve astonishment—I believed that by a *systematic derangement* of my imagination it would be possible to attain the high states of poetic consciousness. The fact that absolutely nothing came out of those trances of mine should have enlightened me, without a doubt. But I thought it normal that the "poesy" did not express itself in any way, and it seemed to me that I felt it in a latent state within me. The rapidity with which all these phantasms disappeared allowed me to measure their worth.

But I lost no time over considerations such as these, nor did I meditate for long on the danger I had escaped in renouncing these illusory practices. For, as I have said, it had occasionally happened that I could no longer master my sick imagination, which sometimes dominated me to such an extent that I had become absolutely incapable of reasoning.

Shortly after Tamara assumed first place in my mind— a matter of a few weeks—my father began to congratulate me on what he called "the awakening" of my "personality." I seemed to be more alert, I looked less apathetic, so he said. These pronouncements finally dissipated what little remorse I had. Visibly, my father rejoiced at seeing me so changed, and attributed everything to my having emerged from "the awkward age." I realized then that he had often worried over my sluggish mind and my sudden fits of abstraction. This astonished me, for I had never thought he attached the least importance to my presence. His delight at the change in me should have given me cause for reflection. But I hadn't the time; I was thinking about something else.

When I say I no longer daydreamed, I mean that almost never now did I sink into a torpor from which nothing could drag me. But though I no longer sought to escape reality—on the contrary, I was plunging into it with delight—when away from Tamara, I often thought of the moments we had passed together, and this, too, comprised a kind of daydream, although its object was infinitely more concrete than the objects of my reveries had formerly been.

Anyway, I no longer needed to construct an imaginary life, for every minute of my real life continued to amaze me with its strangeness. The house in the Rempart des Béguines attracted me as strongly as ever. Each day I analyzed it anew, discovering new details, an angle of stone, a traced seaweed design that I had not formerly seen, a new point of view from which the smile of the immodest naiads varied, becoming ironical or tender, found a forgotten piece of gilding, a worn-down mosaic. I befuddled myself with studying all these things and more. The house had six balconies, four floors, eight apartments; it was nineteen meters high and twelve meters long. I admired the proportions, the daring and grotesque conception, the green color of the marble stairway, and I swore that if ever I were rich I would own a similar house. I would not omit one caryatid or one mosaic!

Then, how can I describe what I felt about Tamara's life? How much I admired her disorder, her unexpected fits of sadness, her amusements. . . .

Sometimes I got up at five o'clock in the morning to go with her to the riding school where she borrowed a horse to ride. We left always before dawn. Supple and determined, striding along in her riding breeches and fawn-colored boots, she was so beautiful that I could have wept with admiration. I remember the nonchalant way she swung her riding crop and the careless way she whistled. The riding school was at the edge of the plain, so we had to walk for almost a half-hour between the rows of silent houses in the deserted streets, where still flickered the street lights. The riding school, however, was in full activity at that hour. By the feeble light of an electric bulb you could see dark forms pass, pushing carts full of forage. I loved the smell of the stables, the sound of the horses snorting in their stalls, and above all else I loved the rustling sound of the hay being moved slowly about with a pitchfork and falling down with a gentle sigh like a receding wave. I, who could think without the least emotion of Tamara as my father's mistress, was jealous of the riding master, whom I hated. Thin, wiry, small, this former jockey, Howard, presented in no wise a seductive appearance. But the minute Tamara entered the enclosure reserved for the riders—while I remained behind the wooden barriers—he ran toward her, calling out in a familiar way that exasperated me.

"Look, my girl, I can't let you have Balzac today! Old Fratt took him out last night and he's tired, nervous, and his mouth's irritated. Take Pompon, or César. César's used to you. Want me to call him?"

Tamara would agree to his suggestion, without appearing to mind his familiarity, and she smiled at the hideous little man in a comradely way she never used with me. They talked about the races, discussed jumps, mentioned competitions in which I would have liked to take an interest but could not because I did not understand a thing about them.

"Here's your mount," he would say. "Put him through some jumps, that'll keep him in good shape for me. There's a good girl! Goodbye, beautiful!"

Then, after giving Tamara a slap on the back, he went off.

She rose smartly in the saddle, made sure of the stirrups, and at the moment she resumed her seat in a crackling of leather, I experienced a pain in my heart as though she were leaving me forever.

"Well, Hélène? What are you doing, still standing there? See you tomorrow!" she would say, and without again looking at me, away she would go at a trot toward the rolling plain of Camp, where she would sometimes ride for hours.

She adored horses. That, too, made me jealous, for I did not understand it. Sometimes she told me to wait for her at the riding school. Her face was always alight with pleasure when she returned, and always, before putting on her jacket, in shirtsleeves despite the cold, she would lead her horse to the stable, wipe the foam from his mouth, give him some affectionate slaps, and talk to him for a while.

Howard liked me. He misunderstood my silence, taking it for timidity, and usually talked to me at such times.

"Your friend certainly likes horses! And she knows how to handle them! It's a sight to see! You know, I let her ride for nothing, all she likes. It keeps the horses in good shape. Not many people come here just now to ride. And it's a pleasure to see her in the saddle. She'd have made a jockey, and a great one, if she hadn't been a woman."

These confidential talks made me uncomfortable. It was as though I were listening to someone talking about Tamara's love life. No, it was worse, for Howard's talk concerned a domain in which I counted for nothing.

V

During the happy weeks that followed, I had only two concerns: how to go to and from the Rempart des Béguines without being seen, and how to prevent my father from receiving the cards being regularly sent out by Mademoiselle Balde's school asking the reason for my absences. I no longer wondered even very much about Tamara's life. With me, she was always self-composed and a little mocking, cutting short with one word any attempt at sentimentality. Sometimes, however, she was sweet, as when she would mingle my reddish-brown hair with her black curls, hiding my face against her shoulder, and murmuring, "Oh, be quiet," in such a tender way that the words were an endearment.

Because she embraced me and was prodigal with her kisses, I was artless enough to think that she loved me, perhaps less than she had loved Emily, but still, uniquely and tenderly, as I loved her. That she never said so, or that at any rate she said so only in moments of abandonment, did not at all torment me. The very strangeness of our silent meetings, the way she showed me the door at the end of them, did not strike me. She loved me, I loved her, we had pleasures together, and that was all that counted in my eyes.

The impressions I had of her sometimes, such as those at the riding school, were very fugitive, and if I recall them now, I may say that at the time I forgot them as soon as they had passed through my mind. I also forgot what I knew about her life when sometimes she remained in bed, smoking, her eyes half closed in a kind of lethargy, her face so expressionless, so indifferent to everything that I crouched motionless at her feet with the timorous respect we feel for the very beautiful when they are dead.

I tried to imitate her, assuming a brusque tone of voice, the somewhat masculine gestures she occasionally made, pretending to despise, a little remorsefully, all the conventions. As a result, I became the object of admiration on the part of my classmates for my daring ideas. But in front of Tamara herself I prudently kept silent. Her ironic smile would have made me want to sink into the ground.

From time to time I had an awakening. When she rebuffed me for a tender word, either with a remark or a shrug, I suddenly realized with bitterness that it was not from me that she would have liked to hear such things. But I quickly banished these thoughts, and if she went on being disagreeable, I naïvely reassured myself. "After all," I reflected, "I don't love her *that* much!"

February came, without the usual rains, and the lawns of the park became green again in a premature spring. When I left home early in the morning to go to school or to Tamara's, it was fresh and bright. The shutters slammed gaily, and everything—from the vegetable pushcarts in the street to the sharp spire of the church, reached by the ascending scale of the roofs—everything sparkled and shone as if painted anew, reflecting small dagger points of sunlight. No longer did gossiping old maids need, for their spying on people, to tilt a mirror at their windows; they could now pretend to be taking a breath of fresh air and, hidden behind their crocheted lace curtains, could survey the passers-by through wide-open windows.

Still preoccupied with his political ambitions, my father no longer limited himself to haranguing the citizens of the neighborhood in some assembly hall or other on Sundays; he was now pulling wires, and I saw less and less of him. Either he was off for a shooting party on the plain, in the company of an influential barrister, or he was taking a boat excursion on the lake with a captain of industry, or might even be driving in the country with a member of the Bar or a president of some society or other, more often than not escorted by a swarm of children carrying fishing rods and sandwiches.

But this tranquillity could not endure, and little by little I felt that something was about to happen. Already, Julia's cousin, the milkman, had innocently told her he had seen me pass in the Rempart des Béguines, and Julia wondered what I was doing in such an ill-famed neighborhood. Already, the Misses Passavent, dressmakers by the day, had begun to ask why it was I returned home so late in the evenings. Already, the verger of the Saint-Charles Church, who lodged in our street, had questioned me good-naturedly: Didn't I go out rather often on holidays? Didn't it take me a long time to come home from school? I did not know what he thought exactly. Maybe he only wanted to put me on my guard against slothful and heedless behavior. At least, that's what he told me. But his questions were put so mysteriously and were so full of insinuations that they gave me the shivers.

There existed a remedy for all this, as Tamara sometimes told me. I could anticipate rumor by telling my father that I was seeing her from time to time and asking his permission to continue these visits. Doubtless he would have made no objections, and assuredly it would be disagreeable for him to learn from others that I had made these visits without his knowledge. However, Tamara advised me so casually to be frank with my father, she seemed so little to fear that something might be discovered—in fact, she had no fear, or rather, she scarcely thought about it—that I let time pass without obeying her instructions. Anyway, I hadn't the courage to broach the subject during the brief moments I spent with my father.

Tamara herself had always so completely neglected to take precautions, and when she advised me to make my confession she seemed so much to be doing it out of a sense of duty, that I was doubly astonished when she asked me seriously if I had done what she told me to do.

"No, I haven't dared to," I replied unhesitatingly, without imagining that she cared in the least.

"Please tell me why you never do anything I tell you to do," she asked sharply. "For months I've been talking about this, and always you put it off! Are you always going to be so careless?"

The irritated way in which she said these words filled

me with consternation. I wanted to explain myself, to make an excuse of some kind, but under her cold gaze I stammered and became muddled. My own fears seemed to me to be ridiculous, and I ended up by averting my face and remaining silent. I thought it unjust of her to reproach me for disobedience, since she had never talked about it except casually. But I felt guilty, nevertheless, for even had she commanded me, I would still probably not have had the courage to confess my secretive behavior to my father.

Tamara surveyed me coldly, and when I paused in my explanations she again spoke.

"I will admit," she said, "that I did not make myself clear until now. But now let it be understood: I give you a week's time in which to tell your little story to your father. And if at the end of the week your father has not heard . . ."

She did not finish her threat, but I imagined she meant to say that she would speak to him herself. That, in fact, was the solution that would have suited me excellently.

"Why don't you tell him yourself?" I replied. I was irritated at the tone of authority she had used, especially since I felt incapable of putting up any resistance.

"One week!" she repeated, without replying. And she began to talk of other things.

Several times during the week that followed, I honestly tried to pluck up courage to confide in my father. But, as if everything were conspiring against me, never had he seemed to be busier: he was always going and coming, making a telephone call, arranging an appointment. . . .

Tamara did not mention it again, and was as affectionate as usual, with moments of silence and coolness such as she sometimes had, but nothing exceptional. I did not worry terribly, then, about not being able to obey her. First of all, I thought her displeasure, supposing she were displeased, would be expressed only in a refusal to see me for a few days, and, while I felt an increasing delight at being with her, I saw her often enough to bear a brief separation.

In fact, being away from her would allow me to think of her and get a perspective on recent events. I also thought that such a separation would make Tamara impatient with all this secrecy and that she herself would therefore speak to my father and so spare me that duty.

I waited, putting off the task from day to day, and when at last she asked, as if negligently, "Well, does your father know?" I started and flushed in such a way that she did not have to wait for my confused explanation. She seemed to reflect for a minute, then made a suggestion:

"If I give you another week, are you sure you'll have the courage?"

She did not look angry. So, still thinking she would eventually attend to it herself, I replied emphatically, "No, I will certainly never have the courage!"

Before I had time to make a move or even to realize what was happening, she had slapped me twice, violently. I was stunned.

Never had anyone struck me before, not even my father. When I was little and my father wanted to punish me, he always locked me in my room. What Tamara had done upset me so that I remained there, choked with angry sobs, trying to catch my breath and to realize what had happened. She looked at me calmly.

"I'm not giving you another week. I'm giving you two days," she said. "And if you don't obey this time, you'll get more of the same!"

Her self-complacency drove me wild. She did not even have the excuse of obeying an angry impulse. She had struck me deliberately, out of sheer meanness!

"No, I'll not obey you!" I cried in a strangled voice. "And I'll go away, you'll never see me again!"

Whereupon, fearing I would become incoherent with tears again, I ran out and banged the door behind me.

In the park, I collapsed on a bench, shaken with sobs, overwhelmed with injustice and misfortune as never before.

I realized that I must go home, but I stayed there, I don't know how long. Then, at last, remembering that it was evening and that Julia was keeping dinner back for me, I started off slowly, being overcome every ten yards or so at the thought of my unhappiness and once more choked with tears, I would lean against the wall to weep before starting on again. Fortunately I met no one I knew, for I should perhaps not have been able to contain myself but might have told everything just to get relief.

As I entered our street, Madame Lucette saw me, became frightened at the way I was stumbling along, and ran out of her shop to call me.

"Why, my poor dear, what's wrong?" she asked, leading me into the shop where, happily, there was no one. I had begun to recover my composure a little, but the words of pity spoken by Madame Lucette provoked a new flood of tears. I could not utter a word. Indeed, what could I have told her? Quickly she closed the door and barred it. Then she led me into the back room. "The customers can just come back tomorrow!" she said softly, looking about for a place where I could lie down comfortably. But there was only a rickety stool and a big rattan chair near the stove, where she was in the habit of resting. Not seeing anything else for it, she sat down in the chair and made me sit on her knees as though I had been a child.

I stayed there several minutes, crying as if my heart would break and at the same time wondering how I was going to explain my grief. At last, moved by I know not what demon, I whimpered pitifully, "My father has a mistress!"

That simple phrase seemed to strike Madame Lucette to the heart. Apparently she considered that a young girl had a perfect right to be shocked and grieved at learning such a thing, and I did not try to find another excuse.

"My poor dear! My poor dear child!" she murmured, hugging me close. I felt that what touched her most was my innocence. The way she saw it, all the turpitude of the world must have been revealed to me when I heard about the double life my father was leading, and she imagined that the memory of my mother added still more, perhaps, to my grief. I guessed all this from the nature of her exclamations.

"My poor lamb!" she said. "Don't cry like that, my dear little angel! So unhappy, and motherless!"

She seemed to address these last words to heaven, which she called upon to witness my misfortune. And thereupon I experienced something which I still recall with shame. My grief was momentarily assuaged, I was almost over my fit of tears, and I realized I must go home without delay, yet, to arouse Madame Lucette to a renewal of pity, I went on lamenting without feeling the least real desire to do so.

"And my poor mother was so good!" I said. "How could he forget her? It all makes me feel as though I were really an orphan, now!"

I secured the hoped-for result: tears came to the charming woman's eyes, just as she was getting up from the chair, having suddenly recalled that I was sixteen and that to hold me in her arms like that was not exactly proper. Again she drew me down against her shoulder and mingled her tears with mine, not thinking of anything else except to console me.

It enabled me for a minute to forget Tamara completely. In the dim little back room, near the roaring fire, surrounded with the good clean odor of paper, pencils, and paste, as I clung with all my might to this pretty and sensitive person who was trying to make me see reason, relaxing agreeably after my violent outburst of tears, I felt perfectly happy and wanted only to prolong this moment of happiness. Heaven knows what awful things I might have been able to think up against my poor father, just to make this moment of beatitude last. But there was no need to talk. Jilted at the age of twenty-two by an unfaithful fiancé, Madame Lucette had grown accustomed to talking about all men as infamous cads. However, while continuing to blame my father's conduct, saying it was a shame the way he left me alone and went running after women, she exhorted me to be brave, to accept everything, and assured me that when my father would be an old man suffering from rheumatism he would be glad to recognize in me the only one who had really loved him and remained faithful.

This vision of my future did not particularly delight me, but I was scarcely listening to Madame Lucette's gentle voice pronouncing these stupidities. With my cheek pressed against her white neck, still damp with our tears, I kissed her from time to time like a child, while she seemed to remain oblivious. She smelled like ink and like a sweet cake. Her round white breasts showed at the opening of her blouse. I felt lulled and pacified, really consoled. And, cynically, I thought it was regrettable that Madame Lucette only felt drawn to me because of my innocence, so beautiful was she in her creamy, smooth, edible way, quite different from Tamara's hard-muscled body. . . .

At last she helped me to my feet and led me to the door.

"Go home now, Hélène. They must be worried about you. I think the best thing for you to do is to behave coldly with your father. Don't talk to him about anything, he would only try to justify himself and you might be swayed, since you adore him so!"

I had never once said that I adored my father, but Madame Lucette had so construed my grief. She had simply concluded that what tormented me above everything was to see my father sowing his wild oats at the risk of losing his soul. I must confess, she had sometimes seen me in church, where I went for the easy intoxication of organ music and incense. The church at that time occupied a great place in my imagination and very little in my moral preoccupations. Anyway, I had almost stopped going after I made Tamara's acquaintance, simply because I no longer needed to seek exaltation elsewhere.

My eyes were dry and I was almost composed by the time I reached home, and I was thinking very little about the future. The silent meal across the table from my father did not affect me. I was still thinking about Madame Lucette, the memory of her was still fresh, and slowly I recalled it in all its details.

I went to bed in this happy mood. The window was open on account of the fine weather. Through it came the sound of someone nearby practicing scales on a piano. It was barely nine o'clock when I went to my room, but, doubtless worn out by my tears, I had felt a curious weakness in my legs and had been obliged to lie down. My bed stood beside the window. For a long time I lay there with wide-open eyes, not thinking of anything precisely, looking out at the dark sky, the lights of the neighboring houses shining behind the lime tree, gleaming through its light leafy tent, turning it into a Christmas tree. I could also see the rain gutter, like a straight, dry tongue along which slipped the shadowy figure of a cat and, far away, on a flat-topped hill, a lonely twisted tree, like one of those twisted and stunted trees of the Orient. Often, in my cross-country walks, I had tried unavailingly to find that tree. . . .

Next morning, before completely waking up, while still in a semiconscious state, I turned and turned in my bed. Confusedly, I seemed to want to cling to sleep, to avoid something that was lying in wait for me, something that bent over my bed, something that touched my face. I woke up with a start. What had given me that impression of something damp touching me? Maybe it was some rain that had come through the window, or maybe . . . When I touched my cheek I realized that it was wet with tears, and the thought passed through my mind: "I shall never see Tamara again." Not for a moment did I recall that the night before I had imagined this possibility with relative resignation. Then, I had even thought of other comforts and pleasures. How had my grief suddenly been re-awakened? Rather, how had these words almost suddenly been torn out of me: "I shall never see Tamara again"? Yesterday they had evoked nothing, awakened no feeling in me. Maybe they were like those wounds which are insensible at the moment of being dealt, and only hurt hours afterward. I could not understand. Those tears I had shed in the park, those tears of rage, of grief, and of shame, they had quickly been dried. I had already known such tears and grief in the past, when my father scolded me or when Julia gave me a rebuff. In fact, it was the grief of a punished child, capable of being soothed by a gentle word. And the night before, as I fell asleep, I had felt peaceful, a little stupefied, but calm. I had not dreamed, nor had I woken up during the night. Yet now, here were these terrible words: "You will never see Tamara again."

I wept much less than the night before, but I walked up

and down in my room, torn with pain, and I lay down and got up again dozens of times. I tried to read or study, but in vain. In an access of insane rage, I tore up an old engraving of which I was fond, saying over and over, "It's not possible, it's not true!" But I had to recognize that it was possible, it was true. And again I felt regret, bewilderment, and suffering. I was angry at myself, angry at my silly words: "I'll go away, you'll never see me again!"— those words I had said to her and which she certainly must have taken seriously. And she would certainly not want me to go back on them. It irritated me, too, not to be able to remember how angry I had been when she had struck me. I repeated over to myself what had been said before she struck me, in an effort to find out what had made me go out and bang the door. And I could feel nothing but new regrets. And fear was added to my despair. Supposing that out of vengeance, not satisfied merely with not seeing me again, supposing Tamara told my father about everything that had passed between us? Supposing he would then keep me in the house or send me to a convent or in some way keep me from ever seeing Tamara again? Never again to see Tamara! But why should I worry about this, since in any case I would never see her again?

At this point I became almost distracted. It was impossible to imagine those days ahead of me without Tamara. I could not bear the idea of going into those streets which had so often led to her, could not think of crossing that park which I had so often crossed at a run to be with her more quickly. The idea of her living so near me, in that house which still existed, was insupportable. I could not accept the fact that she would leave home early in the mornings, just as usual, wearing her riding clothes, and walk alone in the street. I could not think of her taking the train every Saturday to go to the nearby town, could not imagine her lunching on tea and a biscuit, doing everything just as usual, but with me excluded from her life. Wildly, I felt that I could have borne it had a cataclysm swallowed up the Rempart des Béguines and its seductive naiads, the subocean depths of the stairway, and Tamara herself, along with her ridiculous and fragile knickknacks, her African masks, and her raffia mascot doll.

In my mind I reviewed all those little things that she owned and that were crowded into candy boxes or scattered over the shelves, things that had been given her, souvenirs of Emily especially, those innumerable little useless objects, sewing-boxes of mother-of-pearl, pin cushions, manicure cases, perfume bottles, tiny dolls in regional costumes. From time to time Tamara broke some of them, those that no pleasant memory made inviolate, but they were always replaced by others, the small opaline vase taking the place of the Chinese jewel, the glass horse appearing where the porcelain chimney sweep had been. I do not know why her friends persisted in giving her those trinkets which were so out of harmony with her personality. But like a prisoner who can become fond of a spider, she was fond of these things and enjoyed them in moments of weariness.

Oh, Tamara! I mourned each one of those objects, mourned the house, the street, the fresh morning light on

the plain across which you rode, mourned the riding
school and the lean Howard and every one of the horses
you loved—Balzac, Aissa, Hirondelle . . . and the sound of
the hay falling softly, like an unfolded handkerchief, the
light trot of your horse going toward the plain of Camp,
and the sun or the rain on my sudden loneliness as I
stood there by the closed barrier, feeling the emptiness
made by your absence until the following day. I wept over
my own grief, Tamara, when you disappeared as if forever, at those times when you talked to me with willful
cruelty about Emily or when, for no reason at all, you
would say, "No, I shan't be seeing you tomorrow."

But how sweet were those griefs that ended next day
in your arms! For there were your arms, too, your fine
gusts of anger, your cool, slim body next to mine, and
those moments when, in an access of tenderness, you
talked to me gently, covering my eyes with your hand out
of a curious feeling of shame. And there was your hard
mouth on mine, and my ecstasy and yours. I was even
more distraught at depriving you of your pleasure than I
was at losing mine. And I recalled how the usual calm of
your face became suddenly disrupted as smiles flickered
over it and your lips emitted soft sighs and moans, scarcely
audible, while you looked at me with half-closed eyes, as
though drowning in a liquid tenderness, and I heard
again that most intimate cry which I could sense rising
from your innermost being, heard those little cooing
sounds that ended in a lament, as those sharp canines of
yours bit into your pale lip and you were no longer able
to hide your wicked and almost bestial rapture. Yes, all

(80)

this was the burning and poignant and heart-rending core of my love for Tamara. This was the ball of fire that heated our minds; its warmth penetrated us during our walks, during our hours spent together reading by the fireplace, or when we went to the riding school; the plain, the mornings, the river, the house, the sky itself partook of its warmth. The river would have been only a river, the sky only a sky, the morning just a morning, had they not been bathed in this burning light: Tamara's face in ecstasy.

VI

FOR THREE DAYS I was in this inferno. I pretended to be sick in bed with the grippe. My father came to see me, more than usually preoccupied, touched my forehead, found it burning, and advised me to call the doctor. I refused to do so. On the third day I was feeling slightly better, when something happened which cast me again down into my despair. To justify myself for remaining in bed I had complained of insomnia, and Julia, to calm me that night, brought me a cup of lime-blossom tea, slightly flavored with vanilla. In her occasional moments of gentleness Tamara had sometimes made me lime-blossom tea, to which she added vanilla: it was supposed to calm the nerves. Drinking the tea Tamara prepared, I felt a sacrilegious pleasure, since it recalled Julia's preparation which had been for me a kind of incarnation of family comfort. In taking that infusion from Tamara's hands, it had also seemed to me that my restless, timid, and passionate love for her partook in a way of my almost filial love for Julia. So it was that when I saw the cup in the servant's hands and suddenly breathed in that odor, I grew faint and burst into tears.

My fever mounted, and my father declared that whether I liked it or not I must see the doctor next day. By chance, I slept well that night and next day the doctor, upon finding me fresh and rested and only a little pale, dismissed my illness as of no importance and severely ordered me to go back to school rather than malinger in bed.

I obeyed. For several days I dragged myself from home to school, making a ridiculous detour in order to avoid a street or a house that reminded me of Tamara. No longer did I walk through the park, no longer did I go near the boats in the harbor. I no longer loitered in front of the show windows where I used to experience a thousand unavowable desires for all sorts of things—carnival masks, spinning tops, colored marbles. I no longer read, I no longer did anything. At table I was constantly breaking a glass or a dish. I had moments of abstraction when I would get up from table to fetch a clean napkin and, once arrived in front of the cupboard, would completely forget what I was looking for. My father said nothing, but observed me anxiously.

At the end of a week I could not contain myself any longer and decided to go to the riding school. Hoping to meet Tamara, I followed the route she usually took on her way there. But I saw no one except some workmen on bicycles riding silently and hurriedly toward work, their wheels making a sound of wings in the silence. Had Tamara left off her morning rides? Or, to avoid meeting me, had she taken another road? I reached the swing gates and tried to push them open noiselessly, so as to see without being seen. I was afraid that if she were there and saw me she would be so angry that she would scold me in front of Howard. But the gates made such a horrible squeaking sound that Howard himself came out of a stall to see who was there.

"Oh, hello, Mademoiselle!" he said. It seemed to me his voice was less open and frank than usual.

"Is—is Madame Soulerr here?" I stammered.

He surveyed me quizzically.

"No. I don't know if she's coming today. Do you want to wait?"

"No, no," I said, horrified at the idea of the scene that might transpire in front of the jockey. And I fled in a piteous state.

As I reached the corner of the street I suddenly perceived Tamara thirty yards or so away. She had just entered it and seemed to be deep in thought as she walked along toward me, switching her boots with her riding crop. I was incapable of making a move. She approached without seeing me, and in spite of my agony of fear and grief I could not keep from looking curiously at her face, I wanted to see how it looked when she thought she was alone. It seemed less hard, it was full of reverie, there was a flicker of sweetness on her cheek. Was she thinking about me? I almost fainted when she ran her fingers through her hair in that characteristic gesture of hers. At last, when a dozen or so yards away, her eyes rested upon me. She did not even flinch, but continued to advance with the same even gait, looking at me. I would have liked to flee, to sink into the ground; but I could not budge. I was immobilized there against the wall, held by a mysterious force. The idea actually crossed my mind that she might strike my face with her whip, but even that did not give me the strength to move. However, she went by without saying a word, looking at me as though I were an unknown passer-by, and went off toward the riding school. Her hobnailed boots rang on the stones with a clear and pitiless sound. I heard the squeaking of the gates, and then she disappeared. I stayed on there, at the corner of the street, which was still in obscurity, under the flickering street light. At the end of a few minutes, Tamara reappeared, mounted on Balzac, and went off in the direction of the plain without even turning her head to see if I were still there.

All morning long I wandered in the neighborhood like a lost dog, startled whenever a horse came in or went out of the stables, always hoping to see Tamara, hiding myself from Howard, who, I thought, must have been told that she did not want to see me any more. But I did not catch a glimpse of her. Doubtless she had gone off to the side of the plain, making the circuit of the town, following the ramparts and the harbor, so as not to pass by me. Everything was really over.

I walked home. I had left at six in the morning and had wandered in the dusty streets until noon. I was therefore in a sad state, dirty, worn out, and without hope. I longed only for a severe illness that would endanger my life. Then, Tamara, repentant, would come to lean over my bed and murmur, "Forgive me! I did not appreciate your love!" With such reveries I managed to lull my grief until

I reached home where I could go to bed and cry to my heart's content.

At home I found my grandfather sitting on one of the red damask chairs in the dining room, his long legs stretched out, a pipe in his mouth, his elbows on the table.

A fisherman in his youth, my grandfather was now living in retirement with a forty-year-old blond woman whom he called his "housekeeper." He was bad-tempered, purposely untidy, enraged at his enforced inactivity (having lost an arm in an accident), and detested his son who had risen in the social ranks to the status of "boss." He therefore took wicked delight in annoying my father from time to time by an irruption at our house, a visit that was always followed by violent scenes. No one could be more in the way than he was, and he realized it.

"Well, so you're at home, are you? I thought everyone had managed to clear out like they always do when they see me coming. You people have a way of your own to welcome invalids! Where's René?"

"I think he's gone out," I stammered, too surprised to hit upon an excuse, for I certainly believed my father had fled upon learning of the old man's arrival.

"Of course! Anything else would have surprised me! I phoned this morning to say I was coming, and you weren't here. If you'd been, you'd have 'gone out' too, no doubt."

I barely denied this, for I was almost not listening to what he said. I was still seeing Tamara approaching me without saying a word, looking as indifferent as if we had never met, never loved . . . And perhaps she had never loved me, I suddenly reflected. Maybe she had only been trying to amuse herself, to kill time in the long empty afternoons. Maybe she had been making fun of me for a long time. No, that wasn't possible. She had been tender with me, sometimes. One day I had brought her flowers and she had said, "You mustn't do that, you darling, stupid child," with such an intonation of kindness! Another time, she had made me draw up a big list of books that she thought I ought to read. And I remembered something she had said to me once when we were resting, side by side on the divan in the sitting room: "This is the first time I've felt tranquil, my dearest, since I came to this place." She often had called me her dearest, her little oasis in a desert. Yes, she had loved me, I could not doubt it. And I could see us again taking walks together, reading together, her face lit up with pleasure, and I could see again her beautiful hands stamping out cigarettes on the table, or sewing, with the earnest awkwardness of a mariner mending a sail. Oh, and her face, always her face. . . . But how could she, if she had the least tenderness for me, treat me so cruelly, pretend not to see me, not turn round to see whether I was still there, grief-stricken and repentant—yes, I was the one that was repentant! For, try as I would to convince myself that I was not guilty of anything, I deeply regretted that sudden departure of mine and my angry words.

All at once, brusk, logical, unexpected, like a ray of light, an idea struck me: after all, she had not forbidden me to return! That privation had been inflicted upon myself by myself. Why had I not realized, since that dreadful day, that I could go back to her apartment? Because I imagined those categorical words of mine, "I won't ever come back," could not but be taken seriously by her. In saying that, I felt I had pronounced my doom, and my grief, born of the phrase, "I shall never see Tamara again," had been so intense that I had not been able to realize during the past two weeks that I was the one, not she, who had said it. So then—maybe she had waited for me to come back? Maybe she had been as unhappy as I but was too proud to take the first step toward a reconciliation? Maybe she still loved me!

This hope, suddenly revived at the very minute when I believed all was lost, exalted me. Everything could be explained. If, for two weeks, she had been waiting for me to come back, then Tamara had only snubbed me out of quite justifiable anger. She was angry at me for having left her, maybe she thought I no longer loved her—just as I had thought she no longer loved me. I understood everything and excused everything. Even the violence she had used against me, and which had so outraged me, now seemed legitimate. Maybe she had thought that I did not want to please her, that I was ashamed of her, that—no matter what! I was ready to leave the luncheon table, dash out to the Rempart des Béguines, fling my arms around her neck, tell her all about how much I loved her, and about my grief, my stupid lack of understanding. But I could not leave my grandfather, who was sitting there, eating in silence, looking the very picture of reproach.

He ate greedily, wiping his mustache occasionally—

it was too long and got into the soup. But I looked at him indulgently. I was amazed at my own stupidity, amazed at how I had suffered atrociously over something that didn't exist, and already I was almost happy over having suffered so much, since it was over nothing, and since, in another hour, if Tamara had not gone out, I would again experience the happiness I had thought lost forever, and would be all the happier because I could now appreciate my happiness. I looked at my grandfather's big shoulders, at his single hand, enormous and awkward like some strange beast, his wrinkled face, his canny little gray eyes, and suddenly I could not refrain from saying what was in my heart.

"You know, Grandfather," I said, "I'm very fond of you."

He raised his head, surprised. We had never been in the habit of exchanging affectionate words.

"Are you sick?" he asked me, almost peevishly. But apparently he regretted his rudeness at once for, bending down toward me, he added, "Yes, my child, and I'm fond of you. You don't have much of your father in you, sometimes you look exactly like one of our girls." By that he meant one of the fishermen's daughters, and not a daughter of one of the "bosses," the enemies, so I took it as a compliment. But immediately after dessert I made an excuse to get away.

"They're expecting me back at school, soon," I said.

"Oh, I know what you mean by 'school'! Well, see to it that you don't get pregnant, or you know what you'd get from your father!"

(89)

I flushed hotly, I believe, but I did not bother to enlighten him. I felt that the idea of my doing things behind my father's back amused him.

"Goodbye, Grandfather," I said.

"Léna," said he, holding me by the wrist, "if ever you get into trouble, come to see your old grandfather, and he'll fix things up. Now, run along, you good-for-nothing!"

He had never before been so expansive. I realized that I had won his sympathy. It encouraged me, like a sign from heaven.

Without stopping, I ran toward the Rempart des Béguines. And without even casting my usual friendly glance at the caryatids, I climbed the stairs at a run and rang Tamara's doorbell. I rang without thinking what I was doing or without even waiting to catch my breath.

Tamara opened the door after a little while.

My only plan was to throw myself into her arms and let my tears flow. Chance would take care of the rest. But she stood apart from me and I could not follow my impulse but stood there, stupidly, staring at the lines of the floor. Her eyes, usually cold, became filled with an ironic look. But she spoke, I thought, rather gently.

"So, here you are!"

"Yes, I thought . . . I believed . . ." I stammered, unable to explain myself, as I stood there on the landing.

She stepped back to let me enter.

"Come in for a minute," she said.

There I was, in the middle of the room. With the hope of bringing about a reconciliation, I stepped toward the

(90)

divan. But she, seated on an arm of the chair, intervened.

"I forbid you to sit down. Answer me first. Have you got over your little fit of temper? Are you sorry you ran away?"

"Yes," I murmured. Standing in front of Tamara, who was looking me up and down, I felt very ill at ease, and began to tremble lest things were not going to pass off as well as I had hoped.

"You want to come back? As if nothing had happened?"

I nodded.

"Very well. Ask forgiveness."

She was negligently playing with some dice.

"If you want to stay here, get down on your knees and ask forgiveness."

I *could* not. It wasn't out of shame, it wasn't obstinacy, but I could not kneel down in the middle of this room, in front of this person who was looking at me mockingly and asking me to beg forgiveness for something she had done to me. So I stood there motionless, imploring her with my eyes not to demand this thing of me, to realize that I had had enough grief as punishment, if I merited punishment, and to realize that I loved her.

She got up and walked toward me determinedly, and without adding a word, taking advantage of my surprise, she seized me by the shoulders and pushed me toward the door. When I was outside, she closed the door behind me.

I remained alone in the silence of the stairway. A rhythmic thumping sound came from the courtyard. Someone must be beating a carpet. I could stand no more. After so much suffering, this insane hope of mine, and this sudden plunge back into a grief which, this time, would be boundless. She would not go back on what she had said, I could beg and plead as much as I would, her door would forever remain closed to me. Forever.

I rang the bell again. She did not open the door. I pressed myself against it.

"Tamara! It's me! Open the door, I beg of you! I will do everything you want me to do!"

I waited there for a long time in absolute silence. Yet she must be in the room. When I had gone in, the door to the kitchen was closed, and Tamara could not have opened it without my hearing a sound, for that door scraped the floor noisily. So she was there, in the room, on the other side of this wall. She heard my voice—I knew that you could hear everything that happened on the landing in there. And yet she would not open the door! She was teasing me again, she wanted to see how long I would stay there in front of the closed door, imploring her. But the thought did not seem to have much importance. I would not go away without seeing her. I could not go away and have again that prospect of days like the days I had just spent. You can accept grief when you do not know exactly what it is, when it comes as a surprise, falls on you like an enormous and inevitable weight. But when you know all the details of a grief, when you have spent two weeks of it, going through every stage of it— sickness, false hopes, stirred memories, ridiculous and anxious waiting—and when for an instant you have left that inferno behind you, feeling saved, ready to put your lips up to a fresh joy, then one word is enough to make you be overcome by it, then it is intolerable. For then, how can you keep a cool head, how can you reject any sacrifice, or even refuse to sign your own doom?

"Tamara!" I implored. Confronted with that silence, I lost all control. I had to make her respond, I had to see her once more, one single time more. If we must break with each other, it must not be like this, without a farewell, without explanations. Frenziedly I wished she might make a scene, get into a temper, at least accuse me of something!

"Tamara! Open the door! I'll beg forgiveness! I must see you, Tamara!"

Furiously I rang the bell, knocked on the door, whimpered and pleaded. I did not care whether or not the other tenants heard me. Even the thought of Tamara was not very clear. I had but one clear idea, but it was obsessing: that door must open.

"I'll stay here until you open the door! I'll stay here all night long!"

Tears choked me. I went so far as to kick the door, thinking she would open it out of fear of scandal. Finally, at the end of my strength, I sank down on the landing, hysterically emitting inarticulate words, biting my handkerchief, rolling on the floor, banging my head against that wall, that closed door. . . .

Suddenly I was silenced and immobilized: Tamara had come out on the landing. Leaning over me, she raised me up and, supporting me, made me go in, leading me toward the kitchen. All this she did so coldly that I saw she was acting out of sheer necessity. In silence I continued to sob, as my heart continued to pound and I almost strangled with repressed tears, coughing and catching my breath. A tap was slowly dripping. I was afraid, I was ashamed, and every time I looked at Tamara the coughing and sobbing began again uncontrollably. At the end of a few minutes she took me by the neck and, disregarding my resistance, held my head under the wide-opened cold-water tap. At last she released me, waiting in silence while I wiped my streaming face and neck. Then she signed to me to follow her back into the sitting room. There she pointed to the middle of the floor and said briefly:

"Kneel down there."

This time I knelt down without any hesitation. At that moment she could have made me do no matter what.

"Forgive me!" I said brokenly.

She looked at me for a moment.

"Good," she said.

Then she came toward me. I really thought she wanted to torture me still further, that maybe she was going to strike me, and I resigned myself to submit to everything. But she knelt down beside me, took me in her arms, and kissed me, slowly, expertly, deliciously, until at last she had pushed me over backward and I lay in her arms on the floor . . .

Never have I known pleasure more intense than on that day when I thought I had lost her. Never did I more clearly realize the power she had over me and the wicked delight it gave her to use it.

VII

DURING THE FOLLOWING days I tried to understand what had happened and what I had felt, and imagined I could attribute some significance to my feelings during the scene that had transpired. (Later on I stopped preoccupying myself with such things, but accepted them, out of habit.)

I revisualized Tamara's attitude during the quarrel, analyzed the way in which I had let myself be humiliated and maltreated by her. She had obviously taken pleasure in hurting me. I realized that, and sometimes, recalling her expression at the moment when I had at last yielded to her will and knelt in the middle of the room, I flinched again with anger and shame. Yet in her caresses that day, which were more brutal than before and showed more than ever her desire to debase me, to subjugate me, almost to wound me, I found a keener pleasure than usual. And still, just thinking about it, and while detesting the memory and hating her for the look of triumph she had had when she kissed me, I shivered with a strange pleasure. I remembered with shame my own weakness; even while shuddering with disgust and hatred, I had only been able to hold up my lips to hers, and I had melted in a trembling desire for her. Recalling all this, I was still ready to be vanquished once more, I was still ready once again to be taken by her with that delightful brutality.

I had experienced this strange, confused pleasure before, the pleasure of a dual personality, when, at the same time, I regretted not being "good" yet purposely did something wrong. For instance, when I leaned dangerously out from the balcony, or when I read a forbidden book, delighting in these misdemeanors. At church, too, it had sometimes amused me, while listening to the organ, to watch the devout faces of the people who were praying and reflect that perhaps I was the only one there who was not praying. I always asked the Virgin to pardon me for these wicked thoughts, for I had a kind of fearful faith, bordering on superstition. But next minute, my prayer of contrition over with, I again fell into sin, enjoying it, and at the same time being afraid of what I was doing.

But these contradictions never lasted more than a minute, and I did not think about them constantly. The scene with Tamara—which I thought of as the scene-on-the-landing, because it was while out there that I suddenly guessed the lengths to which I would go in order to win back Tamara—was different. Ever since it had happened, this feeling of a dual personality was more tangible, more a physical thing than had been those childish impressions of days gone by.

The character of my relations with Tamara had now changed. First of all, she herself was different after that scene. Perhaps she was merely carried away by old habits suddenly revived—this seemed possible to me, in view of the tone of some of Emily's letters—or perhaps Tamara was stimulated by her sudden discovery of the extent of my attachment. At any rate, our relations were transformed, becoming more passionate, more tempestuous, and also more perverse. Up to then, her fits of temper were dependent, more than anything, upon how many cups of tea she drank or how many packages of cigarettes she smoked, or, later, how much whisky she consumed— she could drink a great deal without seeming to be much affected. Now, since that scene, she indulged in her outbursts gratuitously.

She made me pay for every minute of abandonment and tenderness, capriciously refusing to see me for days on end, putting me to fantastic tests, and when I had obeyed her, instead of welcoming me back to her apartment she would have me meet her in a tea room or at her hairdresser's, where I would be kept waiting for hours, while she had an elaborate manicure or pedicure. Often, too, she amused herself by staring into my eyes fixedly, until I would be obliged to look aside, thus implicitly admitting my inferiority. Sometimes I could hold out for a good minute, but I always ended up by giving way, and this defeat both exasperated me and gave me a confused and indefinable pleasure. She enjoyed demanding my kisses at inopportune moments (as for instance when I was hurried or when she was expecting a visitor) and if I resisted, she triumphed over my objections by force. The very way she took me in her arms, the very methods of our love-making had changed. She forced me to comply to certain refinements of depravity which I would rather have avoided; she described some of Emily's subtleties, with a false pity that stimulated me to a shameful emulation.

Things had reached this point when, one day, my father summoned me to his office. I had never made the confession that Tamara had demanded, she had never spoken about it again, and I thought she had simply asked it in the first place as an excuse to make a scene—such scenes amused her and even seemed to be necessary to her. So then, one day when I was doing some homework in my room, my father sent André to tell me to come down to see him. There was a mocking look on the office boy's face that seemed to bode no good. However, I thought my father probably wanted only to discuss my school reports—although they had remained pretty good of late—or maybe the complaints that had been made about my absences from school.

All the same, I went downstairs rather reluctantly. And as I confronted my father I felt less and less comfortable— the things Tamara had told me about him had only increased our alienation.

I judged him to be hypocritical, on account of his principles; spiteful, because he indulged in the fits of temper of a weak and overworked man; stupid, because he took no interest in the arts; and indifferent, because he was shy and totally incapable of exteriorizing his feelings. In the time that has passed since then I have revised my opinions. I now know that he was endowed with great kindness, but concealed it, fearing to be accused of weakness; that he was sufficiently intelligent, his keen business sense taking the place of intelligence, at any rate; that he was only superficially vain (he was ashamed of his father, he had political ambitions) but was really modest, since he confined his conversation to business and politics, realizing his incompetence in other subjects. His looks played a great part in confirming me in my prejudices: his features were as if crudely carved in wood, his skin was darkly tanned, his hands were enormous, and his self-assured expression made it terribly hard to imagine that beneath this imposing exterior were hidden timidity, sensibility, and tenderness. Only his eyes—rather round, reflective, and of a very light blue, like those of cats or of very young children—gave any hint that my father had something of real humanity in him, but I rarely stopped to contemplate them.

"Sit down, Hélène," he said, as soon as I entered the office.

He seemed preoccupied, fingered that beard of his which he thought so "distinguished." I sat down, worried at these solemn preparations. He remained silent a while, then looked at me without anger but with what seemed to me sadness.

"For how long a time is it now that you have been seeing Tamara?" he asked.

I remained speechless. So far was I from expecting this question that the idea of denying the statement did not cross my mind, even.

"Why, Papa . . ." I stammered.

"Don't protest till you've heard me to the end, Hélène," he interposed. "I don't see you often. Rarely do we have a serious talk. But I think it's necessary today to say certain things to you. First of all, I do not wish to hide from you how I heard about your occasional visits to Tamara. Madame Urson, André's mother, saw you with her in a tea room last week. She thought I should be warned and she added that this was not the first time she had seen you together and that she had questioned the waitress, who said you came there from time to time. Needless to say, I did not congratulate Madame Urson upon this investigation carried out by her but instead reproached her for gossiping and told her it was not my habit to have you spied upon. But that's not all. Here's a letter I received. Read it."

He held out to me a thick sheet of paper. I took it with a trembling hand. On it were typed these words:

Sir: You aspire to become a deputy of the Liberal Party, you go to church and you send your daughter to church, in order to get into the good graces of respectable people. But you will not be elected if all the town finds out—and in Gers, things become quickly known to everyone—that your daughter assiduously frequents the Soulerr woman, your mistress, and the neighborhood of the Rempart. God only knows what she is doing there! Your father already lives with a whore. A fine family! If you wish to follow the advice of a friend, lock up that shameless young daughter of yours in a convent, send your old father to die elsewhere, and try to do without your mistress. If not, you will be unpleasantly surprised at

(100)

*the coming elections! And if you don't want the whole
town to know this, send two thousand francs to
General Delivery, Rue des Cuillers, number . . .*

I did not take time to read the address that followed.
The letter was unsigned. I was overwhelmed.

"If I had given you permission to visit Tamara," my
father went on, "or at least if you had kept me informed,
I would never have shown you such a disgusting thing.
I wouldn't even have gone to the trouble of speaking
about it to you." Taking the letter and putting it in a
file, he went on, "The minute one has a rather prominent
position in the society of a small town, such things are
only to be expected. But I want you to become aware of
the meanness of people and I want you to realize how
painful it is to me to learn of your conduct in this manner."

He waved his hand to prevent me from interrupting.
But he need not have worried: I was too afraid of what
he might now say to be capable of uttering a word.

"I myself urged you to meet Tamara," he continued.
"I did so because I judged her worthy of being known
by you, no matter what they say about her in this town.
I also do not consider that you are very guilty in enjoying
the acquaintance of a person whose exciting life, intelligence, and charm may have aroused your curiosity. I do
not consider it a great crime that, at your age, you may
from time to time stay away from school to have a cup of
tea with a woman friend—for I have learned that it is
during school hours that you have been seen in that tea
room. There's nothing very serious in all that. What is

(101)

serious is that I trusted you utterly, and you have, by your actions, destroyed my confidence in you. Never did I ask you, no matter at what hour you came home, why you were late or what you had been doing. I thought—since you did not tell me anything—that what you were doing was of no importance. You may think me naïve, perhaps, but I was convinced that, in matters of importance, you were open with me. But that you went of your own accord to see Tamara—for Tamara would be incapable of inviting you to come to see her without your having asked it of her and she would otherwise have told me about it—that you did this without telling me, absolutely destroys my confidence in you."

He waited a while to see whether I felt the need of replying, but seeing my look of utter dejection, he went on:

"I will say no more about this letter. Obviously, I shall not reply to it. And as soon as possible, I shall appear at some public function or other with both you and Tamara. I do not want people either to imagine that you have been seeing her at my instigation or that you have been permitted by me to see her in secret and not in public. It is necessary that I do this; but by doing so, I may compromise my election. I hope you will reflect on this fact and that in future you will conduct yourself more reasonably."

I thought he was going to end with these words and, relieved, I half stood up to go, when he went on in a low voice, as if hesitantly:

"Hélène, I have known all this for several days. That

I did not speak about it sooner and that I do not punish you is because I have reflected and now realize that I am partly to blame for your not having behaved openly with me. You may have—yes, you may have doubted my affection for you, my interest in you. I have not taken your mother's place, that's certain. And my occupations have not allowed me to watch over you as closely as I could have wished to do. But—well, the other day I remembered something. Oh, it may seem stupid to you—and you yourself most surely do not remember it. One day—it was when you were twelve, maybe, or even less, I don't know —you came to me very seriously to confide something to me, making me swear I would never speak of it to anyone. You said that a little girl in your class had cheated at an examination. You wanted to know whether or not you should tell your teacher about it, Mademoiselle Barjasse was her name, I even remember that. Of course, the whole affair was quite unimportant. But this affair was important to me. There you were, with your serious little face, look' ing at me, confident that what I would say would be absolute truth and justice. I mean, you were so sure I could not make a mistake. . . . I remembered that incident when I received this letter and while I was listening to the absurdities of Madame Urson—whom I sent packing, by the way—and I was sad, Hélène."

He reflected a moment, and it seemed to me that his eyes were shining rather strangely. But I had scarcely listened to what he said, so relieved was I that he knew no more than this about my relations with Tamara, and that he was not going to take some terrible steps against me. Yet this conversation should have been one of the most important events in my life, since it showed me that my father loved me, and proved at the same time that he was worthy of my love. Seeing my lack of response, he sighed.

"Let's not talk any more about it. But Hélène, my dear child, I am going to make one more request. I ask it of you without anger, and I assure you I ask it with a real desire to make you happy. Please try to explain what impelled you to call upon Tamara in the first place, and tell me how many times you have met and what you talked about. What I am asking for is, in fact, a full confession."

He softened the last word with a rather sad half-smile.

I seemed to detect, in all this, a feeling of remorse for having left me so much alone, without moral support, and I at once had the idea of exploiting this feeling. Somehow, I must secure his permission to go on seeing Tamara, for I could not face the contrary. To sway him, I would have to use hypocrisy, deftness, and conviction—all of which I felt capable of putting into play. It was only a question of lying.

I began by confessing, as the most likely thing, that I had paid that first visit to Tamara simply out of curiosity. I went on to say that I had soon realized that her mind, her conception of life, did not correspond to the rather bohemian aspect of her apartment. (At this remark, my father flushed, probably thinking that I had been rather astonished at the idea of him in that "bohemian" setting.) I went on to say that I had told Tamara about my lonely life, that she had given me advice, lent me books, and had eventually helped me with my studies.

"But for that you must have had to see her often?" my father queried.

"Several times a week," I replied, this time without dissimulation. He would eventually learn that my visits to the Rempart had been frequent. As I saw his reflective look I thought he was doubtless meditating on the fact that my school reports had been considerably better, that I had been more talkative and had indulged less in fantasy, and that everyone had remarked upon my improved appearance.

"And—did she talk to you about your studies?" he asked, not without astonishment.

"Yes, often," I asserted emphatically. My father sighed. No doubt he was reflecting that for a long time now he himself should have been taking an interest in these things. How could he reproach me for having sought elsewhere a consolation which he had not given me? However, I saw that so much solicitude on Tamara's part astonished him and that he was not as reassured as he would like to be on the quality of her influence. I must convince him at all costs. So, pretending to speak unconstrainedly and as though moved by his gentleness to confide in him, I exclaimed, "And then, too, Papa, we could talk about clothes, things like that! I never see anyone and I don't know what clothes I ought to wear, what things are becoming to me. And it's no fun to read or to study when no one encourages you!"

Every one of these words must have struck home, for

he was suffering from a bad conscience, that I knew. So I went on to explain as best I could what Tamara had done for me, what she still could do, always trying to emphasize her good influence, the wisdom of her advice, the good results that could be expected from my association with her.

My father listened attentively. At last he stopped me with a wave of the hand.

"My dear, that's enough. Thank you for explaining yourself so frankly. I must reflect on all this, now. All I reproach you for is your secretiveness, but I begin to understand now why you did all this behind my back. You thought, maybe, that I would forbid this friendship; you were afraid of losing it. But I hope that if you had realized how wrong it was of you and how you would hurt me by such actions, you would have abstained."

"Oh, yes, Papa!" I said, shedding a few tears. "Don't think that I went there because I did not love you. It was only because you hadn't time . . ."

"I've often regretted it, believe me, my dear. But working hard, making a fortune and a position for us in the world, that, too, is thinking of you. Do you understand?"

"Of course, Papa," I sighed, in such a way as to convince him I would have preferred him to have thought about me in a more direct way.

At last he dismissed me, with a final request.

"Hélène," he said, "promise me one thing only. I myself will talk to Tamara about this, for I want to find out from her if you may not, without realizing it, have bothered her more than she could have wished. Stay in your room this afternoon. Think about the effects on me that your secretiveness will have. Think about how you could have spared me all this by talking to me openly. Think about the gossip of Madame Urson, about this letter and how much it has hurt me. I'm sure you will understand the seriousness of your conduct and that you will resolve not to repeat it. That's all I ask of you: one afternoon of reflection. I do not forbid you to see Tamara again. I will only try to find out to what extent your visits are agreeable to her. You may go now."

I believe he was expecting, after the few tears I had just shed, at least a word of excuse or a gesture of affection from me. But I went out without saying a word, so amazed and happy was I to have got off so easily. I went up to my room almost dancing with joy. Tamara would certainly not fail to back up my statements and from now on I would be free to go to the Rempart des Béguines without any fear of being seen. What astonished me above everything was my father's innocence. He had suspected nothing of our relations. I did not realize that such amorous relations were, after all, not very frequent, at least in respectable regions such as ours, where many people must even have ignored their very existence. Without going as far as that, my father's narrow-mindedness inclined him to label all such deviations maladies, and to believe they could be detected on the faces of those affected. I am sure he had never imagined it was possible, in the respectable town of Gers, to meet people afflicted with such vices. At any rate, I am sure he thought he would have perceived it at once in any of his acquaintances.

(107)

So it was that I spent a very tranquil afternoon, not in contrition, as my father had hoped, but in a peaceful reverie. The effort I had made to convince my father of the good influence exerted over me by Tamara had made me look back upon our acquaintance and I asked myself what, indeed, had been her influence on my poor mind. My conclusion was that it had not been so bad.

To conquer a last vestige of remorse, I recalled those former torpid states of mine, that strange feeling of split personality which I no longer had, and I told myself that, being thus transformed, I could not be very guilty. I had not entirely lied when I said Tamara had given me advice as to the books I should read. She herself read a great deal, her preferences being either for frankly erotic books or classic works, the drier the better. She read very few novels. Whenever she felt nervous, she would plunge into some passages of Descartes or Pascal, or even a book on geometry, amusing herself in solving problems as though they had been cross-word puzzles. In fact, as far as I was concerned, whenever I saw her reading about proofs of the existence of God or discussions on "actual and sanctifying grace," I knew a storm was brewing and that I had better beware.

Needless to say, I did not share such reading with her, but there were other books that she did make me read with her. The most commendable of these was the *Liaisons dangereuses*. That book, at least, had an effect which I considered wholesome: it liberated me from a Wertherlike sentimentality, toward which my Germanic origins inclined me all too strongly. Had I followed my own inclinations I would have treasured souvenirs—bits of ribbon, half-smoked cigarettes—and would have looked at a star each night at the same time as did my beloved. Tamara took a high hand with such budding sentimentality, demonstrating its absurdity.

Due to this direction of my literary tastes I became infinitely superior to my classmates, who could think of nothing more daring than to go out with a boy and get kissed in some dark corner. And how contemptuously did I listen to Madeleine, for instance, who confessed such things to me in the schoolyard, beneath the old pear trees. Poor Madeleine! She was always in love with some college boy or other, always was first at a rendezvous, always was there with a smile on her dull, freckled face, ready to make way for any prettier and more coquettish girl who came along to devastate, with one smile, the week-old love affair. She was always forgotten even before she had ever counted for anything. I could just imagine how, later on in her life when she was the wife of a humdrum civil servant or shopkeeper, she would no doubt manage to turn these dull deceptions of her youth into romantic heartbreaks. It would be her way of filling up the empty Sundays when her husband sang in the choir or presided over a meeting at the rifle range. No, Madeleine hadn't a chance of ever escaping Gers, the little shops, the Monday roast, and the Sunday mass. Her life would flow calmly in the channels set for it by the trees of the park, the municipal theater, the lake and the plain; it would always be colorless and filled with boredom.

Poor Madeleine! I could never say anything other than

that to her tales of woe. I thought of my own future, of my liberty to come—I was so sure of "escaping" eventually —I thought, in the long run, of Tamara, and the thought flooded me with a hard radiance, a reasonless plenitude, a freedom of movement so intoxicating that I sometimes had to flee, singing at the top of my voice, in an effort to wear out these new forces. Tamara had given me this fugitive inebriety, this appetite for living and feeling, in exchange for my countless and complicated daydreams, my vegetative indifference. I might not be able to determine whether she had been good or bad for me; but at least, only rarely did I think of her with regret.

VIII

"Hello, darling," Tamara said, giving me a kiss. "You see, when you try, you can be really clever!"

I looked at her interrogatively. I was never sure when she was serious. Often she was making fun of me just when I thought she was being most open and frank.

"Why, of course, I mean with your father!" she went on. "I saw him yesterday afternoon. You have quite convinced him that our knowing each other is useful to you! He even thanked me for having, as he put it, pulled you out of a worrisome state."

She burst out laughing, seeming to be very gay and completely relaxed.

"You're a good child. Come, kiss me."

With this, she drew me down beside her on the divan, and I pressed my head against her breast. She stroked my hair as if she were stroking a cat, and as a matter of fact I was almost purring with pleasure.

"My good child . . . my sweetest . . ." she whispered, with a tenderness to which I was no longer used. Suddenly she bounded up. "I'm going to dress!" she said. "He left me a pile of money. We'll go to the flower market, we'll fill the house with flowers, to celebrate!"

Leaving me a little bewildered, she ran to the bedroom. I was not used to seeing her so gay, but the idea that this gaiety came from the fact that she could now see me freely gave me so much pleasure that I forgot for a moment the embarrassment of that word "money."

As we went out she ran down the stairs so quickly that I could barely follow her and before we left the house, as we reached the downstairs hall, she kissed me on the cheek vehemently. In the street she put her arm around my shoulders as we walked; I tried to fall in with her long, easy stride. The sun shone. We walked down to the harbor in the fresh breeze and the good fishy odors. The market comprised a number of cabins, made of woven rush, their counters overflowing with flowers as far as the middle of the pier, and we were caught between the parapet and these perfumed waves of bright flowers. The lake was fern-colored, and almost motionless.

There were dahlias, especially, violet, red, purple, the color of blood, of storm, of crushed pomegranate; there were lilies, stiff daisies, pompously simple, and little bunches of forget-me-nots, poppies, round bridal bouquets, sweet williams of a sumptuous red but hairy like caterpillars. All these flowers left only a narrow path on the pier through which we walked, stopping from time to time to look at the lake and the distant mountains or at a sailing boat exactly at our eye level, with brown- or orange-colored sails. The wind stirred my hair, fluttered Tamara's short curls. With her long, lithe body, her corolla of hair, she herself seemed to be an exotic flower, a brown flower, spicily perfumed, and containing some sweet poison.

A fisherman called out to her from his boat, suggesting that she go for a sail with him. She only smiled, queening it over the water, the carpet of flowers, the ancient worn stones. And sometimes, with half-closed eyes, she threw back her head as if drinking in the sunlight.

We bought some dahlias, some big double marguerites, some lilies, and also, farther along, some sulphur-yellow sunflowers, with black hearts smelling like the ashes of poplar trees. Then we sat down for a long while on the stone flange of the pier, looking at the water. It must have been about ten o'clock in the morning.

"You'll stay to lunch," said Tamara. "Your father has given permission. I explained that it was bad for you always to be alone while he lunched at his club."

I adored her for saying that. She was holding in her lap a long sheaf of flowers and she looked, in her yellow blouse, like a dazzling idol, a Mexican or Incan goddess in a temple lost in the jungle, full of precious stones and serpents. And on my shoulder she laid her hand, that brown, hard, lined hand of a haymaker, not at all the hand of a sexual pervert, but rather a hand made to lie on the neck of a horse or the hip of a woman, with its fingers a little too flat, a little too supple, evoking the hands of Chinese torturers.

To myself I simply said her name, "Tamara." And every time it rose to my lips like a prayer, I was suffocated with a sudden tenderness. At the end of the pier some ladies were coming toward us. What did it matter if they saw me sitting there in the sunshine with Tamara? I had the right to do so, now. And if they turned their heads

(113)

aside so as to avoid seeing her as they passed, I, too, would be enveloped in their disdain, which would bring me still closer to her. I almost wanted this to happen. But the ladies did not come nearer than the first flower merchants, and we remained alone.

"One of these days we'll take a sailing boat and sail all around the lake. Would you like that?" she asked. "How nice that would be, in hot weather, to spend several hours on the water."

I could only press her hand in reply. She seemed not to notice the sailors and the women who passed from time to time, looking at us with astonishment as we stayed there motionless on the parapet, in the sunshine. And so I, who usually was afraid of being noticed or of being jeered at, I, too, remained oblivious, feeling marvelously protected.

Before leaving, we bought some more flowers: a little bouquet of poppies, and several bunches of rush which Tamara wanted to strew on the floor of the apartment. Then we went slowly back, following the narrow little streets of the lower part of town. It was dark and cool there. Some children were playing in the dust.

Silently, and I believe happily, both of us, we reached the Rempart des Béguines. Tamara sent me off to a grocery store to buy some canned foods, while she arranged the flowers. When I entered the apartment I was amazed at the extraordinary aspect of the flower-decked room, the violent colors of the dahlias and sunflowers mixed, and the rushes strewn on the floor. Lounging on these rushes, we lunched on the things I had bought, tuna fish and pineapples, in the strong perfume of the lilies. The weather was already hot, and when I raised my eyes above those flowers that Tamara had placed in vases on the floor to look out at the sailing boats going off over the lake, I was lost in a boundless wonder. We remained lying about like that for the better part of the afternoon. Naturally I should have been attending several classes, but I did not even think about it. Instead, I tried to sketch Tamara, making several drawings, one of which pleased me. From time to time I sighed with happiness, also with fear that this happiness would not last.

"Tamara?"

"Be quiet," she said, in that rather husky voice of hers.

And she drew me down beside her. From her hot skin rose the smell of burnt grass, of moss, of mushrooms in the forest. She breathed in the heart of a poppy which, she said, smelled exactly like an apricot; and she bit into it.

"Tamara, supposing it's poisonous!"

"I don't believe in poison. Are you afraid of it? Are you afraid to kiss me after I have eaten poppy?"

It was another challenge, as usual. But she spoke so tenderly that I flung myself upon her, pressing my lips against her pinkish-mauve mouth, which was impregnated with the bitterness of the poppy. I did not want to know the reason for this renewal of tenderness. I thought of several bad reasons: violence had become too monotonous, a surge of sweetness would restore its piquancy; or else, maybe, she was gentle with me because of the money my father had given her. . . . I repelled these thoughts. Tamara was there, all sweetness, pressed against me, and all was well.

That evening she accompanied me almost all the way home. As we passed near the park, we leaned over toward the water a moment. Behind us, the street lights in the avenue were lighting up, and the little flames reflected in the pool made it look like a giant birthday cake with several rows of candles, or like a crystal palace lit up from inside, and, imprisoned there, I saw with astonishment the reflection of our two faces. While still near this water, Tamara gave me a rapid goodbye kiss. And she said, as she turned to go toward the Rempart, "I wish it could always be as it was today, darling."

Coming from her, that phrase was almost an excuse, and it completely overwhelmed me.

Shortly after having authorized me to see Tamara, my father must have been greatly puzzled, for the series of bad school reports, which for some time had lessened, again stacked up and my father had some rather desperate discussions on the subject with Tamara. She told me about these, laughingly.

"Is it possible," he had asked, "that she is again falling into a kind of lethargy? I can't explain it, for she seems gay and wide awake."

Tamara had reassured him; it was just a passing phase, she said. Before, it had been sheer incapacity that had caused the bad school reports, now it was laziness. The poor man had said, "I almost hope you are right!"

In fact, laziness held me in its grip. Apparently Tamara had sworn to make me happy—I wondered for how long. I was constantly amazed at the ease with which she could transform herself. For a few weeks she was all gentleness, all sweetness. She did not say one hard word or make one violent movement. Her face radiated goodness, her flexible voice remained almost singing, it was the very voice of love. So much so that its modulations tore me to shreds and made me say to her sometimes with tears, "Please, be still." To which she would reply only with "Yes" in a tone that clearly indicated she had understood, a tone that was the epitome of sensitiveness and delicacy. She had genius, at such times.

Suddenly she seemed to understand everything, feel everything. "Darling," she said one morning, "I'm sorry always to leave you alone when I go to Howard's. Would you like to ride with me?"

I was astounded. "Of course I would!" I said. "You never asked me before, and so . . ."

"I never thought about it, darling. But the idea came to me a few days ago and I have already thrown out a word to your father on the subject. You ought to speak to him about it, too."

In my inmost self I well knew there was a lie in what she said. I had asked Tamara more than once, timidly, I'll admit, if I could not accompany her on her rides and she had replied with very little kindness, saying she had no wish to teach horsemanship, that she liked to ride alone, and that, anyway, my father would certainly object to my practicing a sport as unusual as horseback riding was in Gers. But I was much too happy to think of reminding her of these words. Anyway, she would have serenely denied them, maybe, for her conception of truth was extremely vague, as I knew.

In a few days, as if by miracle, there I was with a

complete riding outfit, and I tasted the pleasure of walking with Tamara through the deserted little morning streets, without the prospect of having her leave me at the stables. My father, contrary to what Tamara had previously affirmed, was delighted that I wanted to learn to ride, and my grandfather was even more so. He had said, "At last she's going to become somebody," and my father had smilingly approved his gift to me of a superb riding whip. Tamara objected to my learning to ride at the riding school. She seemed never to want to be separated from me now. "Howard, you can give her Hirondelle," she said. "He obeys my voice, and I'll teach her. This child can learn to ride very well in the plain." Howard, not very enthusiastically, yielded to her request, and so there began a series of wonderful rides in the country.

I would have liked to know the name of every tree, every bird, every insect, and I now brought back to my room, instead of books and engravings of which I always quickly tired, a cricket in its little cage, a bouquet of flowers for my father, a bird that would sing each morning in the big dark house, which had become singularly bright, as if freed from a spell, as my father himself said, since flowers and birds had acquired the right to be there.

I was crazy about my horse, Hirondelle. For nothing in the world would I have changed horses each day as Tamara did. I loved the hot summer days and the crickets that seemed to make the air even more oppressive with their cries. I suddenly loved the coolness that came at five o'clock in the narrow streets. I loved the unexpected fine summer rain that fell in the dust and I held out my hands to it. I loved my brand-new happiness of that summer. But above all else, I loved Tamara. Tamara was the short grass, the hill, the white thirsty prairie, the rain and the dust, the coolness, the sunlight. Tamara was the pleasure of the mornings, the prostration of hot noon in the shut room, the delicious sadness of five o'clock, while the fresh breeze from the lake rose toward the windows as the glorious sun set, looking like a ripe, juicy orange.

Suddenly, all of Tamara's asperities had been put aside. Banished were those angles of her character that she had, in the old days, purposely sharpened, and no matter how far I let myself go in tender overtures, no longer did I encounter limits to her indulgence, comprehension, and affection. This new easy-tempered way of hers troubled me sometimes. Why was she like this, now? Why? Had she not loved me until a certain moment? No, she said, she had always loved me as she now did. But why this new tranquillity, this purity, almost, this love of nature, this tender and melodious word, this pleasure which was less precise, as though melting in sentimentality? At the end of a few weeks I could barely recall my frenzies of bygone days, or my former perversities, or the darker pleasure which had its aftermath of detestation. Tamara encouraged me in this forgetfulness by her whole attitude. If I reminded her of something in the past, she would raise her eyebrows in a great show of innocence. The Marquis de Sade? *Les Liaisons dangereuses?* Those things had never existed! Rough and violent treatment? She had been a little nervous, that was all. And if I persisted, she would say, "Darling, surely you won't hold it against me that at certain moments I was impatient?" Her voice was so suave as she spoke that I was inevitably reduced to tears. Then she would reason with me.

"Why, what are you crying for, exactly? Aren't you happy? Don't you love me any more?"

No, that was not it. I wept because I suddenly felt she was playing with me, that she would cry out as she used to do—as she used to do only six weeks before. She was going to say, "Now, enough of this fooling! Go home!" But she did not shout this, she remained angelically charming. When she wanted me to go, she said, "I want you to rest a little, darling. Don't you think you should? You won't be too sad? You're sure? You know, if you feel lonely, you can stay here. I didn't really mean what I said."

This was what frightened me, this perfection of manners, this supreme refinement that obliged her to add a series of "You're sure? Really? Tell me if you don't want to," and so forth, to any simple request I would have obeyed with pleasure.

This solicitude of which I was the object was flattering, but it sometimes almost turned into obsequiousness. There was something about it that I did not quite grasp, something from which I was almost excluded. But aside from these moments of discomfort, I swam in an ocean of happiness. The proof of it is that I almost did nothing now but draw pictures of Tamara, some of them rather good, in my opinion. However, at that time, I had to sidetrack several letters from Mademoiselle Balde to my father, informing him that I no longer went to school except once or twice a week and that this would have brought about my dismissal had it not been for the esteem in which he was held.

All the same, I sometimes recalled the other Tamara. There was that day, particularly, when we happened to hear over the radio the same melancholy song that had marked the beginning of our relationship. Tamara was sitting in a leather armchair, her arm around me, her hand on my shoulder. I looked at her stubborn profile, her short curls, her broad shoulders, all that deceptive and equivocal virility of hers. Suddenly her hand closed on my shoulder and she murmured, almost exactly on the note that had just died out, "Do you remember?" That tone was so exactly *right*, it so exactly suited the poetically smoky and perfumed atmosphere, the calm and melodious music. But at the same time, it was so absolutely *false* that I was startled and shook myself free of her, almost roughly.

"What's got into you?" she said. The brief question relieved me of a great weight. I almost wanted her to fly into a temper. But she went on immediately, "Are you nervous, darling?" And again I felt ill at ease.

For of what could I reproach her? Obviously, I could not reproach her for her kindness! I wondered if I were not regretting my former unhappiness, my tears, my shame, and my uncertainty. No, of course not. Yet even so, Tamara's violence, the way she had of sharpening her claws, of enjoying and exaggerating her cruelty, it all added up to a virility which made me suffer, which I resisted, but to which I finally succumbed in a kind of mental spasm.

I repeated over and over to myself that I was happy.

A hundred times I had wished for this close intimacy with Tamara, and now I had it. Every other day we went riding. I no longer remained alone, forsaken, standing there behind the barriers. We lunched together almost every day, with the awnings down, because of the heat. Then we lay down together in the silence. Flies hummed. From time to time we heard the voice of someone passing in the street or on the quay below. We drank tea, Tamara smoked without talking. And only toward five o'clock did we arouse ourselves.

I never went back these days to see Madame Lucette. Indeed, I avoided going there, and when I went along the sidewalk in front of her shop I saw her watching me reproachfully, as she dealt out her pencils and stationery. Like everyone in town, she certainly knew that I was seeing Tamara. Perhaps she was saying to herself that either I had been a thorough hypocrite or had, as she would put it, "made a pact with the devil." Sometimes she ventured a little nod of the head, a vague gesture which might be interpreted as a summons, an attempt to call my attention—doubtless out of a wish to sermonize me in the back room of the shop. But the fugitive emotion I had formerly experienced with the beautiful bookseller was completely gone, and anyway, aside from pretending once again to be full of despair—a difficult thing to do—what could I expect of her now, except words? So I merely replied to her salutation with a rather constrained smile as I entered the door of my house as quickly as possible.

Then, on top of everything, my father had a personal telephone call from Mademoiselle Balde, informing him that I no longer set foot inside the school. In an amusedly indulgent way he asked me a few questions. Did I wish to go to another school? Had I any complaint to make of anyone or anything at Mademoiselle Balde's school? Was there, after all, some serious reason why I played hookey so persistently? I replied as best I could that there was no particular reason, it was just that the Balde school bored me, that I preferred almost anything to the paved schoolyard and the monotonous classes there, that certainly I preferred riding, sketching, and idleness.

Fortunately my father had only the vaguest ideas on the education of young girls, holding only to the firm conviction that all a good wife needed to know was how to read, write, and sew. He therefore smilingly replied that he quite understood my point of view, but that, all the same, he could not authorize me, at sixteen, still not having "come out" in society, to leave such a select school, deliberately, and spend my days doing nothing. He added that he was not scolding me, that moreover he would soon study the question of presenting me to society, but that in the meantime he requested me to attend at least one out of two classes and said he would write to Mademoiselle Balde, asking her henceforth to consider me merely as an "auditor."

This time I embraced him wholeheartedly, delighted with the phrase which almost authorized me to do nothing at school except put in a few hours there each week. Incidentally, my father added that he would take me next week with Tamara to an exhibition of painting at the mayor's residence. This would help me get accustomed to appearing in society. He had given Tamara a sum of money, he said, that would allow both of us to appear in new outfits.

Having disposed of all this, my father disappeared into his oak-paneled office with the majesty of a wizard who, having fulfilled his mission, retires into his shadowy grotto.

IX

Tamara joyfully welcomed the idea of the exhibition. She, who had lived in Paris, pretended thoroughly to despise the social events of our little town, but the receptions at the Vallées were, as a rule, extremely elegant, and Tamara, despite everything, was flattered that Madame Vallée could consider inviting her.

"I don't really see why they invite me since they have always acted, ever since I came here, as though they didn't know me," she said, with assumed ill humor. And the very next day, contrary to our custom, we went shopping for clothes.

Choosing our costumes proved to be difficult. Tamara seemed to be as interested in my outfit as in hers. What was needed was a light toilette for an exceptionally hot month of May. Anyway, we heard that the reception would end in the gardens of the house; after the exhibition, the Vallées would retain their more intimate guests, and my father and Tamara would be among these. I was not mentioned on the invitation card, but my father had decided to take me along. No matter what, I should make my debut in society that year.

Tamara ended up by choosing for me a sleeveless dress in a pretty green taffeta, the full skirt having several thicknesses of tulle beneath it. Certainly it was a pretty dress, but I felt it was not quite the thing for Gers. However, I was delighted with it for I almost never wore anything but my plaid-trimmed navy-blue school uniform. At last I would look like a real young lady!

When I tried on the dress, Tamara decided my hair-do was too childish, so she discarded my net and arranged my hair in a thick knot at the nape of my neck. I was dazzled at the results. I thought I was as beautiful as the motion picture stars in American magazines; almost—oh, sacrilege!—as beautiful as Tamara. I discovered that I had pretty shoulders, big eyes, regular features, and a much smaller waist than any of my classmates. Bundled up in my school uniform or in my childish knitted things, I had never perceived these facts. Tamara seemed to be as delighted with my looks as I was. "I was sure you'd look wonderful! Green goes so well with your reddish hair! You are divinely beautiful!" she said.

To complete my outfit we had to ask my father for a little more money, explaining to him that perhaps it was necessary for me to have some high-heeled slippers, silk stockings, and a big garden-party hat. Also, it would have been a shame to wear this marvelous taffeta-and-tulle dress over ordinary linen underwear. Tamara simply could not tolerate such a thing! So she went from one thing to another, using feminine wiles I would never have suspected in her, looking at lace-trimmed chemises and panties, arguing over hem-stitching and insertions with the skill of one who knows all about such things. It was as though I were going to have a wedding. At last I possessed three complete sets of pure silk and real lace lingerie, and I felt that from one day to another I had become the dictator of feminine fashions in Gers.

As for Tamara, she was going to wear, with a wide black tulle skirt she already owned, a new yellow silk blouse—she was fond of that color. It was lightly brocaded in the same tint, giving an exotic look to the silk, a look accentuated by the very short sleeves cut on the bias and by the high neckline, something like that of a Chinese tunic. A wide sash of the same silk completed her costume.

"You'll have to be careful not to stay too close beside me," she said smilingly. "This yellow and that green don't quite go together."

A few days before the reception, my father asked to see my dress. He seemed to be delighted with it. I believe he did not have a very clear idea as to how young girls should dress; during his eight years of being a widower he had forgotten about such things. As for me, I knew that none of the other girls who would be at the garden party would dream of wearing a sleeveless dress, but I was rather proud to be doing something out of the ordinary.

All three of us—my father, Tamara, and I—were rather ignorant, in fact. We had no idea what we were risking by going together to the exhibition and reception at the Vallées'. For not only would we be running the risk of making my father lose the coming elections, we would also be risking banishment, all three of us, from every salon in Gers. People might henceforth cross the street to avoid speaking to us. From that day forward we were risking becoming pariahs. My father, although very strict on certain points—he never missed going to church, he always wore a hat, he never failed to send flowers to his hostesses—was quite ignorant of some of the elementary rules of social intercourse, even in Gers, where he had been a prominent figure for almost ten years. He had not observed that he had been forgiven quite a few small lapses on account of his sizable fortune. But to take his mistress to a party to which he had been kindly invited, to offer her his arm in the street, and to be accompanied by his daughter who, on purpose or not, had been omitted from the invitation—this comprised a challenge.

As we entered the long room where the exhibition was hung, my father, as usual, energetically pushed through the throng toward the mistress of the house, who, dressed in red silk, was perorating at the far end to a group of young painters and old gentlemen, the latter being civic officials, members of the Entertainment Committee.

Around us I felt a rather marked movement of surprise, but I attributed it to my own beauty, or to our rather showy elegance, and I was convinced that it was flattering.

The crowd separated at our passage so that we traversed the long room between two ranks of curious people, and were thus carried upon a wave of humanity to the very feet of our tutelary goddess.

More aware than we were of what was going on, she had quickly grasped the situation, realizing why the crowd parted before us. She hesitated only for a moment as to what stand to take.

Madame Vallée had reigned over the society of Gers for

many years, and she was bored. Her tastes in everything were followed. The local newspaper devoted long articles to her receptions, her clothes, her favorite men friends—for she had some. One after another, she had favored a young musician who played the organ, a romantic and "progressive" abbé, a Scotsman, a hunter, and a bridge fiend, and an army officer, who had died in the war and about whom she never spoke, even in her husband's presence, without wiping away a tear. Successively, the best society of Gers had been mad about music, religion, bridge, and fencing. Madame Vallée had recently made painting fashionable, in honor of a fair-haired youth who was now swaggering beside her, his purple tie swearing disagreeably at his Egeria's dress.

But Madame Vallée's prerogatives had their inconveniences. No sooner had she vanquished all resistance to one of her crazes than she would get tired of it and, moreover, she had to maintain the fearful admiration of her subjects by constantly renewing her acts of bravado. Thus far this year she had sponsored a hat that was like a peasant's bonnet, had favored boating parties, and advocated monkeys as household pets. It was not enough. So, confronting this spontaneous withdrawal from Tamara, a movement that outraged her because she had not given the signal for it, she decided to make Tamara fashionable in Gers.

Taking three steps forward in the midst of the silence—the people who surrounded her were obviously expecting one of her crushing sallies—and with a face contorted in an effort to be suavely at ease, she exclaimed:

"My dear Noris! My dear friend! It's such a long time

(129)

since I've seen you! How are you? And so this is your beautiful friend—Madame Soulerr, I believe? What a lovely costume! And what is your Christian name, my dear girl? I can call you that, for I am ten years older than you!"

Tamara, astounded at this unexpected greeting, murmured a few unintelligible words. The lady then turned to me with the same enthusiasm.

"And your young daughter! I'm sure you brought her here to present her to society. How pretty she is, and what a lovely dress she is wearing. Young girls ought always to show their bare arms!"

Having enounced this subversive maxim in a loud, clear voice, Madame Vallée judged that she had done enough for me and my father and abandoned us while she bore Tamara off toward the old gentlemen of the Committee.

"Come, my child," she said to her, "I'm sure you don't yet know these gentlemen? They will be delighted to make your acquaintance." And they disappeared in the compact throng, while my father and I stood as if paralyzed. My father quickly pulled himself together.

"What a charming woman!" he murmured with satisfaction, but still without realizing how much had been at stake during those few minutes. "Come, dear, let us have a look at the paintings."

And we, too, entered the crowd, which closed behind us, now that we were recognized members of the select society.

Seemingly not impressed by the rather funereal setting,

the guests crowded about the buffet or, as discreetly as possible, followed the servants who were passing platefuls of refreshments. These seemed to be provided in abundance. No doubt, for economy's sake, and so as not to be obliged to invite everyone several times, the opportunity had been seized to exhibit five or six paintings by young artists to whom certain hopes had been held out. Between the plumed heads of the ladies, risking the anger of hands armed with minute sandwiches and sticky little tarts, platters that were being passed full of glasses and champagne bottles, you could occasionally have a glimpse of a corner of a frame. I was able to note that the frames of the blond youth's paintings were elaborately carved and gilded, while the frames of the other paintings, the works of artists who had been invited at the last minute, were of plain black wood.

In the distance I could see Tamara, still under the aegis of Madame Vallée, eagerly surrounded with people. Near her I noticed a man of thirty or forty years of age who was wearing a turtle-neck sweater and who seemed to know her well. He was not very tall but had the broad shoulders of a deckhand, a big, chubby and happy face, and a mouth which, when he laughed, opened from ear to ear—it was the face of a real faun.

"Who is that gentleman, Papa?" I asked.

"Which one?"

"The one in the sweater."

"Oh, yes! That's Max Villar. Hasn't Tamara ever talked to you about him? He's an old friend of hers, a painter. You should go over to her, I'm sure she'd like to introduce you, and I have a few words to say to the president of the Liberal Club."

I had no time to protest that I hadn't the least desire to be presented to Max Villar, nor to point out that Tamara seemed to be completely uninterested in me. My father had already disappeared. So, very slowly, I went toward Tamara.

"Oh, there you are, Hélène! Where is your father?"

"He's gone off to talk to some president or other. He said you would introduce me to this gentleman."

"That's so! You don't know Max, I'd completely forgotten it. Well, here he is, Max Villar. Hélène Noris."

Without much enthusiasm I gave my hand to the artist. Why couldn't Tamara say three words to me without prevaricating? She knew very well that I had never met Max Villar! We had talked again about him only the night before. She had then, without meaning to, revealed that she still saw him occasionally, and it had been a disagreeable revelation for me. From the very beginning I had got used to the idea that my father came to the Rempart des Béguines. There was a kind of fatality about his being a part of Tamara's rather dreary life. But that she went on seeing this artist who had saved her from a life of misery, as she willingly admitted, and that he was still perhaps her lover, considerably upset me. I could accept the fact that she was my father's mistress; because it was my father, perhaps, I did not imagine anything physical between them and their relations seemed to be almost legitimate. But in front of this man who was laughing with her, who held her by the arm, who talked to her familiarly, I almost felt hatred rise in me.

Why had it to be this man, to begin with? This stocky fellow, with the face of a faun and big laughing eyes. I could not keep from imagining those eyes looking at Tamara, my precious Tamara, and his big workingman's hands caressing her. He was not even handsome, he never stopped laughing, and he laughed in a way that I judged not very intelligent. My father was much more imposing, with his tall figure, his tanned face, his blond beard. I almost went so far as to become indignant that Tamara was unfaithful to him. What would happen if he found out? She had never yet confessed any physical relations with Villar, but her very reticence had made me suspicious, and now that I saw them together I could no longer have a doubt. They were whispering jokes to each other, laughing in an understanding way, and they stayed there together. While my father did not suspect anything, but artlessly believed that this individual was only a "good friend" of Tamara!

I stood there saying nothing, my arms hanging at my sides, embarrassed in the midst of all these people who did not know me, and not knowing what to do with my hands. I did not dare take a cake, for fear of spotting my new dress, nor to smoke, for that would not have been admissible in this society. At last Tamara seemed to become aware of my embarrassment.

"Max, be a darling. Take care of this child who is bored to tears. Lead her over to the buffet, introduce her to some of those young men. In other words, see to it that she has some fun. Will you?"

"Of course, of course! I'm always delighted to be of service to young ladies!" he replied with a loud laugh.

I was furious. Not only did Tamara not talk to me, she disdained taking care of me and in addition rendered me foolish in the eyes of this mocking artist. She obliged him, who had not the least desire to do so, to "take care of" me, as she put it. And he would perhaps not have obeyed her had he not still been her lover! I would have much preferred to stand there against the wall, not knowing what to do, than to be obliged to talk to this unattractive individual.

He led me through the crowd to the buffet, a long improvised table decorated with flowers that, already withered, were drooping their heads over a few dried-out sandwiches. I drank a glass of champagne at his insistence, and he himself did not seem to disdain the rolls and sandwiches that remained.

"What a jam! Are you among the favored few that are going to be admitted to the hanging gardens of Babylon?"

"I think my father has been invited," I replied as disagreeably as I could.

He did not seem to be affected by my contemptuous tone and went on, between polite phrases, engulfing cakes and tarts with a persistence worthy of admiration.

"I'm going to be at the garden party too. I believe there's some champagne put aside for it," he said reflectively. Then he again burst out laughing. "You don't look as if you're having a good time, I must say! But you're wearing a very pretty dress, all the same. Did Tamara choose it for you?"

"Yes!" I replied, with completely misplaced vehemence.

I could not bear to hear the name of Tamara pronounced

with such familiarity, and I was not at all grateful to Max Villar for his efforts at conversation, made solely for the sake of Tamara, that Tamara he loved so much. This time he seemed to be struck by my animosity, for he put down in an absent-minded way a cake that he had just bitten into.

"What's wrong with you, young lady? Something upset you? Were you expecting to see someone here who hasn't come?"

I shrugged.

"Oh, see here, don't be sad. I'll stay with you, that will give you countenance, and standing here you can watch the door. If the darling of your heart comes in, all you have to do is run toward him and leave me to less ethereal pleasures."

This time I felt ready to burst into tears. This was the limit! These idiotic pleasantries, that tone . . .

"I'm not expecting anyone," I said in a choked voice. "And I beg you to leave me alone!"

He now looked at me seriously.

"So then, you must have something against me? Do you really want me to leave you alone? I'll go and see if I can find Tamara."

No, that was not what I wanted. I still preferred to have him stay there with me.

"No, no," I stammered, "don't go away, please don't."

He seemed to be astonished.

"If you're acting like this to vex me, you needn't go to the trouble! I'm not angry at all. I understand very well

(135)

that people sometimes prefer to be alone. I'll go see if Tamara . . ."

Couldn't he let one minute pass without saying her name?

"No, don't go to find her!" I exclaimed, at the limit of my suffering. I felt a tear roll down my cheek.

Max Villar took me by the arm and drew me into a corner.

"So, you're in love with Tamara, my child," he said gently, interrogatively.

"Yes, of course I love her," I replied without reflection, blowing my nose and wiping away my tears, hidden from suspicious regards by Max's broad back.

"Oh, so you love her," he said slowly. I realized too late what I had said, and flew into a temper.

"Yes, I love her," I said, disregarding all discretion. "And I know you're in love with her too, and I detest you, and . . ."

"Careful. Speak softly, someone may hear you! There's the trace of a tear on your cheek. Here, let me." And he skillfully wiped my face with his handkerchief, while I held back my tears with difficulty.

"So you detest me, do you?" he went on, after a minute, when he saw that I had calmed down.

I flushed, but said nothing, my outburst being over. Oh, how I wished I had not said those stupid and compromising words! And how could I take them back? Knowing Tamara as he did, Max Villar could not help but understand them.

"Well, my child, it's ridiculous to be jealous. Especially

of me! Tamara, I swear it to you, Tamara only considers me a good friend. She doesn't have the least bit of love for me."

Was he trying to make me believe that she had never been his mistress? But I knew she had been, she had told me! Seeing my incredulous look, he corrected his statement quickly:

"When I say she isn't the least bit in love with me, I mean really in love, of course. Sometimes she manages to have little moments of weakness for me, but I swear it's of no consequence."

I no longer had a grudge against him. Evidently he was doing his best to comfort me. He did not realize that I was ready and eager to welcome a lie; he had said that Tamara occasionally had "little weaknesses" for him, seeming to take this lightly and not realizing that the words were heartbreaking. I looked at him, puzzled. He was gay, he had broad shoulders, big hands, the face of a faun or a sad clown, his thick chestnut curls were in wild disorder. There was nothing remarkable about him, in fact. Did Tamara love him? If not, why did she give herself to him from time to time? My father kept her, she pretended she loved me. What place in her life was reserved for Max Villar? I sighed, and he patted my back with awkward sympathy.

"Listen, now. Stop being upset. With Tamara, it's certainly useless," he added, a little sadly. But immediately afterward he began to laugh again. "She's in high favor today, is Tamara! She must be delighted! I'm sure it would spoil everything for her if she knew you were sad. Pull yourself together. You are ravishingly beautiful and Tamara loves you."

I smiled at him in spite of myself. He was right, there was nothing to cry about.

The stifling atmosphere had lifted a little, all the same. Some of the guests had discreetly withdrawn, and Madame Vallée had already mysteriously let a series of old gentlemen pass into the garden, along with them the entire Entertainment Committee. My father reappeared at the door, obviously looking for me.

"Oh, there you are! How do you do, Villar?"

Again I was seized with indignation as I saw Max Villar cordially shake hands with my father, apparently not embarrassed in the least. On the contrary, he seemed to think the encounter rather amusing.

"Hélène, Madame Vallée has sent word that you may go into the garden. The other young girls have already gone out there, and she wants you to make the acquaintance of some of them. Run along, dear."

The idea of making the acquaintance of the well-bred young ladies was not at all pleasant. I had only begun to recover my composure, and I would have preferred to stay in some corner, unseen. My father went toward the far end of the room, from which a door led out directly to the terrace and the garden. The guests who had been invited to stay had gathered in a group, while the others quickly took leave with rather tight-lipped expressions. The artist guided me out toward the terrace.

"Cheer up!" he whispered as we went through the doorway. "Tamara is very fond of gaiety!" And he gave me a comforting little wink.

(138)

The terrace and the sloping garden were admirably situated, halfway up the hill, a little higher than the Rempart des Béguines, commanding the same view of the lake and the low houses of the fishermen but overlooking several levels of streets with rooftops shining in the sun and some tree-planted avenues. All the "best society" of Gers were there in the magnificent but rather small garden. Madame Vallée had excused herself to the undesirables by apologizing for its size. "Our garden is unfortunately so small! I had to invite the Committee, the members of my husband's club, the choir, and you simply would not find room out there now. But sometime soon I'll manage to find an opportunity . . ."

To the favored guests, she had declared this was the only garden party she intended to give that year.

From the terrace I could see the whole garden, two round lawns, where had been set out some chairs, parasols, and two buffets just like the one in the dining room. Surrounded by a group of eager old men, Tamara was gracefully posed on the edge of a chair. Farther off, my father and some members of the Liberal Party were drinking white wine and arguing, with much waving of hands, probably over the plans for the town festival of lights that would soon take place. I had found a chair a little off to one side, to avoid those young ladies whom Madame Vallée wanted me to meet, and I was admiring Tamara. She looked like a fashion plate, so elegant was she, so slender did the wide sash make her seem to be, so enhanced was her complexion by the yellow of the high-necked blouse. She raised her eyes toward Monsieur Vallée, who was talking to her, and as she tossed back her curls a feeling of sadness overwhelmed me at the spectacle of all this femininity in her that I had never noticed before.

The afternoon, with its soft May sunlight, passed slowly by. The dresses of the ladies became rumpled as they sat on the grass. Dancing began. On the terrace, Tamara was dancing in my father's arms, under the malevolent gaze of a plump young widow, Diana Robel, owner of a cloth factory, who had been trying for two years to captivate him. And I saw Tamara dance with one after another of the Committee, always with the same grace, the same radiant smile, displaying all her aerial charms to the tune of a Strauss waltz. Tomorrow, everywhere in Gers, they would tear her to pieces; the ladies would criticize her dress, her behavior, the original cut of her hair, her impudence—she had come in on my father's arm, she had not worn a hat! She had dared to dance with all the important men of Gers! But this afternoon she reigned over the garden, the ramparts, the town. Everyone wanted to dance with her, and she seemed never to tire but accepted every invitation, dazzling in her yellow blouse—such a daring color, they would say. She danced with the fair-haired youth of the purple tie, Madame Vallée encouraging them with a wave of her hand. Never had Madame Vallée had such a lively party; this being so, it did not matter to her that Tamara was not wearing a hat.

I, too, danced. I danced with a young artist in a cowboy shirt, who discussed his future while waltzing with me. Then I danced with several mustached college boys who felt impelled to whisper in my ear that they were members of the Liberal Circle, to which my father belonged. To keep myself from being too much affected by all this attention, I had to recall my father's fortune, thanks to which I was what is called a "good catch." My hat, my high-heeled shoes, my low-cut dress had unleashed this offensive of amiability; they seemed to announce the fact that henceforth I was on the marriage market.

In addition, Tamara's presence brought up the thought that my father, in order to go on more freely with his dissolute life, would be far from sorry to get rid of his daughter as soon as possible. It was only up to me whether or not I would have, during that very week, three or four proposals of marriage. But I was not out for such proposals. While dancing near Tamara, I tried to attract her attention, and I smiled bravely at her, without feeling much like smiling. I began to suffer from a slight intoxication, due to the waltz and to the numerous refreshments brought to me by my dancing partners, and sat out a dance with an old gentleman, who said he was a friend of my father and who talked to me about painting for a long time with singular ardor. "You have a face that one would like to carve in stone," he said, adding, "And at sixteen! What freshness! No, surely, with a face like that, you can't possibly admire the symbolists' paintings?"

While talking, he pressed my hand in his, and I dared not make an effort to withdraw it. Decidedly, Max Villar had resolved to take the place of providence in my life, for he arrived just in the nick of time to ask me for a dance and to tear me away from the enterprising old gentleman.

"Little girl, watch out, you must take care with these patriarchs here! One minute more and he would have suggested taking you for an evening sail in his private yacht!"

Van Berg was also there, going to and fro, carrying glasses of champagne and plates of cold meats to all the ladies under forty. I avoided meeting his eyes; for I recalled that visit I had made to his office, when I had asked him such naïve questions and when he had asked some less naïve, which I had only understood later on. I could see that he expected to talk to me, and whenever I saw him coming toward me through the crowd I tried to avoid him. But in front of my father I could not refuse his invitation to dance.

As he carried me off, his gaunt face was lit up with malice. My father had said, "By all means dance, my child. I think that after this number it will be time for us to go home." Van Berg took me out on the terrace in the midst of the dancers, and he held me very close to him, so that my efforts to free myself were vain.

"You're very pretty today," he said. "Why didn't you ever come back to see me? I'm sure you still have a lot of questions to ask, haven't you?" His mocking look made me flush.

"No," I replied shortly.

"Well, then, you have learned a lot since your last visit," he said. He did not labor the point, but his words were enough to sober me completely.

As we left, Madame Vallée accompanied us, maintaining her enthusiasm at its highest pitch right to the threshold.

"Au revoir, dear Noris, au revoir, sweet little Hélène, darling Tamara. I hope to have you all again here, soon. You have done much to make this little party a success! Au revoir. We shall meet again, soon . . ."

We were on the point of leaving the house when we were rejoined by Madame Périer. This lady had always treated Tamara rather indulgently, but being a rival of Madame Vallée and less fortunately situated in society, the protection that had just been extended to us offended her as though it had been a personal injury. She therefore decided on the spot that she would treat Tamara with no respect and, feigning not to see her, spoke to me as she went out: "Don't forget my ball, June 17, Hélène, dear. Aline is counting on you. And so you can both come out at the same time! If your father will accompany you and serve as escort, he will be more than welcome!" Having thus clearly indicated that, at her house, at least, Tamara should not be seen, she left without waiting for a reply from my father, who was frowning with anger.

Tamara had not made a sign at this public insult which several people had overheard. But when she was seated in the car, at the end of a moment of silence, and while we were slowly going down toward the Rempart des Béguines, she suddenly pressed herself against my father's arm and wept.

X

Surprisingly enough, Tamara did not seem to brood over this annoying incident. She was perhaps a little nervous during the days that followed, but our life went on as before. There was, however, that day when she went off to the riding school without telling me and I learned next day that she had gone riding without me, but I ascribed this to a rather natural desire for solitude, nothing more. Then, there were some shopping excursions, in preparation for my first ball. This time, Tamara did not show much enthusiasm over choosing the new dress and wrap I had to have for the occasion. She was again having her spells of sadness and depression and again—something that had not happened for some time—was drinking tea at all hours and smoking several packets of cigarettes a day. Also, she began taking me for aimless walks about the town, hunting out places for which I did not understand her predilection. We would spend hours, for instance, at the Crémone tea room, a nondescript, quiet, and deserted place, frequented only by old Englishwomen. The tables there were of gilded wood, hideously carved and painted, the curtains were of yellowed crocheted lace, the mirrors were blurred and dim, the carpet on the floor was frayed. A frightful sadness hung over these remnants of better days. There were two waitresses, as old as the ladies who generally haunted the place, and they went about their work in silence. Tamara would remain there in the semi-darkness, seeming to like the hushed atmosphere, while I tried to pass away the time in reading the menu, an old yellowed card, decorated with a quaint vignette representing a lady seated at a table in a bower and lifting to her lips a glass of bluish liquid. Under this picture was an imposing list of things much in demand by way of refreshment: *Glace à la rose, Glace silésienne, Glace Grand-Perron, Glace aux amandes* . . . There were a good thirty of such ice creams listed, but you could never get anything but a pale lemon ice smelling of beeswax.

I preferred Ford's Café to the Crémone tea room. Ford's was down by the harbor where we often rested after a walk. It was pleasant to go down the three steps to reach it, on a hot day, and to find yourself in an icy-cold little cellar, sitting at tables of black marble. More often than not, we went there toward four o'clock, when there weren't many people. The cellar smelled of beer and fish, but the proprietor never failed to bring Tamara a tall glass of iced tea, with ice cubes in it and a slice of lemon floating like an aquatic plant. Sometimes we went there to lunch on fish fresh from the lake, and Tamara would enter into conversation with the fishermen, mingling her drawling and gentle voice with their voices, without anyone's seeming to find it out of place. I remained silent, happy to feel her living there near me as though she were alone, waiting for her to tell me, with a nod of the head, that it was time to go, and happy to have her lay an imperious hand upon my shoulder as we went out, followed by all eyes.

Yes, that was the way I preferred her to be; not violent, but calmly authoritative, letting her always active will weigh lightly upon me. Her moments of abandonment acquired a greater value when waited for in a vague and submissive uneasiness, and the anxiety that her excessive tenderness had caused vanished before this nostalgic silence which restored to her all her mystery.

She had left off that gentle, refined, and imploring tone of voice. I liked the categorical firmness with which she would declare in the shops, "No, not pink. I don't want to see you in pink!" I liked her to make the decisions as to our amusements and books, and I, who entered into revolt at the very idea of my father's being able to forbid me something, enjoyed obeying the prejudices of Tamara.

However, this period of calm was not to last. One evening, upon arriving at Tamara's—she had asked me to go to the moving pictures with her—I experienced a painful shock at seeing Max Villar sitting there drinking whisky.

"Well, well, here's my little friend," he said, smiling. And turning toward Tamara, he added, "You certainly like them young! She's just a baby!"

This way of talking about me displeased me profoundly. Also, he was in shirtsleeves and did not excuse himself for it. I was pained that he went to no trouble on my account but treated me as a negligible quantity, and I was all the more pained that Tamara seemed to encourage him in this behavior. However, I hoped that the meeting was accidental and that Max Villar, who did not live in Gers, would soon have to leave in order to catch his train. But almost immediately Tamara shattered this hope.

"Would you mind going to the movies with us?" she asked me.

"Not at all," I automatically replied. All the same, she might have consulted me before inviting Max! This was my first thought. But then it suddenly struck me that *I* was the one being asked to accompany *them!* It was as though I were the superfluous one. Max noticed the disappointment on my face.

"Just think," he said, "you see her every day, and I don't even get to see her every three weeks!"

After all, he was really rather nice. But seeing him there near Tamara, hearing him talk to her in an intimate way that revealed everything, made me suffer. I was sure he tried to keep back tender words and familiar gestures so as not to hurt me. But in spite of my jealousy I could see that, as far as Tamara was concerned, there was no question of tender affection.

He dined with us, resting his elbows on the table, emptying a bottle of wine without an effort, joking about everything. I learned that he was talented, made money, spent it quickly, was always without a sou, that his only property consisted of a room in the capital, a little house in the country, and this apartment, which he had inherited from his father.

"He was a funny old man," said Max, "he adored living here because the house had a bad reputation. He said that living here, surrounded by whores, kept him in good condition. But nowadays, I never see anyone in the stairway except respectable working-class people or charming ladies with veils, which would seem to indicate that since my father's time the house has gone up a step socially, so that almost nothing interesting goes on here except maybe the usual amount of bourgeois adultery. In a way I'm sorry, for my taste inclines more to the preceding tenants. I'm not saying that to please you, my darling beautiful Tamara."

She laughed without seeming to be annoyed. They were paying no attention to me.

I was becoming jealous of Max. Would I be able to keep from being jealous of my father? How could Tamara cold-bloodedly put me into such a situation as this? After all, maybe she was doing it on purpose. . . .

Max Villar did all he could to make the evening pleasant for me, but his kindness only made me feel Tamara's hardness all the more. At the cinema he insisted that she sit between us, and twice I saw him withdraw his arm from her hand. And I, who so loved to be with her in a theater, holding her hand discreetly, feeling her leg against mine, this time found the film atrociously long, for she did not once look at me during the entire performance. Only between shows, as she ate an eskimo pie, did she condescend to speak to me. "It's a marvelous film, don't you think?" she asked, in such a totally indifferent way that I could not force myself even to agree with her.

Without stopping to think what I was doing, I accompanied them to her apartment. My father knew where I had gone, he would not be worried if I came home late. I may also have hoped that, after Max had left, Tamara would have a tender word for me. We all went upstairs together. Tamara served some iced drinks in the tall yellow Venetian glasses of which I was so fond. The conversation dragged for a while. Max Villar seemed to be embarrassed, but finally asked a blunt question: "Aren't you afraid to go home alone through the park?" Then only did I realize that Max was going to spend the night at the Rempart.

For a second I tried not to believe it, giving him a look of desperation. He turned aside. As soon as I had left he would no doubt rise, go over to Tamara, and take her in his arms. He would do what I had wanted so many times to do, he would sleep with her, would wake at her side, would look down at her sleeping. . . . No matter how much I told myself that obviously he did not consider things so romantically, I could not resign myself to it. But the most intolerable thing was not his presence, not the idea that Tamara was unfaithful to me or loved someone else, nor even the quite frightful feeling of my sudden loneliness. What hurt me most was to imagine the kind of love they made together, to imagine Tamara . . . It seemed to me that she was lowering herself, that she was gainsaying everything I admired in her: her hardness, her energy, her mocking superiority. But now, here she was, she had a lover like other women had, a lover that she kept at her side not out of interest—which was, I thought, why she endured my father—but rather out of some queer feeling of gratitude, of affection, maybe of desire. If so, then she was not as different from other women as I had imagined. Otherwise, how could she take pleasure in a love-making that she did not control, in which she did not play the dominant part? Could it be that she experienced with that stocky, curly-haired young man the same pleasure in submission that I experienced with her, a submission of which I was a little ashamed? I did not want to believe it. Rather than imagine her thus fallen from glory, I preferred to accept the painful thought that she was keeping Max there out of sheer perversity, just to reduce me to despair.

At last I stood up to go. "Au revoir," was all I could say as I looked at him. He opened his mouth, to say something amusing, perhaps, then thought better of it. "Good night, Hélène," he said simply, then sat down and poured out another glass of whisky.

"Good night, darling," said Tamara lightly. "Telephone me tomorrow noon."

The door closed behind me.

I walked all the way home, through the tepid night. Once there, I went to bed and cried for a long time, with a kind of bitter pleasure. I almost felt as if they were not my tears, as if only a superficial part of me were suffering and crying, while inside my head my brain was ticking away, like a well-regulated watch. I tossed and turned on my rumpled bed, my pillow became damp and my cheeks scalded with tears, I bit the sheet to repress my cries. And every time the thought of them came, every time I visualized Max and Tamara together, imagining them as they were that exact minute, my tears flowed again. "One of these days," I groaned aloud, "I'll get even for all this!" I did not realize that this desire for vengeance is only still another form of love.

Next morning I could not resist going to the Rempart des Béguines. I simply had to see Tamara after this night, spy out on her face the signs of a moral failure, some trace of female flabbiness which would allow me to despise her and recognize in her a sister as frail and weak as myself or anyone.

Max opened the door.

I had not expected to find him still there at eleven o'clock in the morning. But not only was he there, he was still in pajamas, his hair rumpled, his eyes red with sleep, the jacket of his pajamas gaping open, showing a hairy chest.

I stood there petrified. But he grinned widely.

"Come in, child. Tamara's not here."

I followed him into the bedroom, a little embarrassed, but determined to wait for her to come back. She must have gone out to buy some milk or bread for breakfast, I thought. I would stay there to catch the first expression on her face, find out what she looked like when I was not there. Would she be a little languid, a little tired and indifferent? I wondered if she would have that closed look of her bad days, or the charming look of melancholy which sometimes clouded her eyes, or a smile that I had never seen, but which would be my revenge if I could glimpse it for a moment, that shameless smile of a woman . . .

"Sit down, for goodness' sake. After all, you're at home

here too," said Max, stifling a yawn. "Excuse me for look-ing like this. I just woke up. I was sound asleep when the bell rang. If it hadn't been you—I saw you through the peephole—I'd never have opened the door, I'd just have gone comfortably back to bed. When our friend got up this morning I didn't even hear her. Not to keep you guessing, she's simply gone for a ride on the plain."

"She's gone to the riding school?" I exclaimed, unable to hide my astonishment.

"I've just told you so, sweet child. Don't go away on account of that. I've got a lot of things to say to you, I was turning them over in my mind while I slept. Yes, yes, I assure you. But first of all, I must have a spot of break-fast, I could never talk correctly before breakfast. The conversation we are about to have demands a little feeling of relaxation."

Systematically he put a glass, then a bottle of whisky, then a packet of cigarettes and an ash tray on the low table.

"Very good," he said, contemplating his arrangement with satisfaction. "A very fine still life. You standing there in front, me picturesquely shaggy. It's an allegory that hits you in the eye: the beauty and the beast. Vice in bedroom slippers ogling a bottle, standing beside Virtue in sandals and a blue linen dress. I assure you, we make a very fine picture."

The news that Tamara would most likely not be home before noon—if then, for she sometimes lunched on a sandwich with Howard—had made my visit meaningless. But it would have been sad to go away now, and I still hoped she might come in unexpectedly. Also, Max turned out to be entertaining. Like many provincial artists, he suffered from the fear of being out of date and out of the limelight. So he went to the extreme of eccentricity, posing as the typical daubster, although he was really worth much more than that, for he had talent. His jesting, his rather too professional vocabulary, his pea-jackets, his generally sloppy look, were all a part of this pose that was calculated to astound the respectable citizenry. I will say this for him: these ridiculous attitudes accounted for more than his talent in getting his work appreciated in Gers. His paintings were bought because his looks made people believe in him: he looked like an artist; at the very first glimpse you could see he was a real artist. Even I myself, while vaguely realizing that something in this assumed character of his rang false, could not help but be impressed.

So I let him persuade me to make myself comfortable on the divan.

"You have probably saved a shipwrecked man," he said, pouring out a glass of whisky. "Just have a look at the love letter our charming friend left for me." He took from his pocket a scrap of paper on which I recognized Tamara's heavy handwriting, and held it out to me. "I'm off to the riding school," I read. "I don't know when I'll be back. Don't answer the telephone and don't open the door. But if I find you still in bed, I'll throw a bucket of water over you. And don't think for a minute that worrying about the parquet will stop me. I kiss you—oh, just on the forehead! Tamara."

All of Tamara was in that note. I recognized her gentle mockery, her affected indifference. But it did not enlighten me as to her true attitude toward Max. She might just as easily have written it to me. It revealed nothing, except that she evidently did not *adore* Max, but this I already knew. The last phrases upset me, all the same, as Max perceived. Taking back the paper, he drank his whisky at a gulp, refilled the glass calmly, then turned toward me.

"My child, I don't want you to be unhappy," he said. Then, shrugging, "Listen. There are a lot of people who are in love, miserable, and worthy of pity. I don't worry about them. You must not think I'm in the habit of mixing into other people's affairs. If I take an interest in your affairs of the heart, which happen to coincide with mine, it's got nothing to do with charitable feelings."

He got up and went toward the fireplace, took from the mantel a bundle of papers, and said, "Here, this is the reason I'm interested in you. Your little drawings. You see, the minute someone goes in for sketching, I'm interested. Of course, these are horribly bad. A sure line, but all wrong, the perspective is frightfully distorted, and as to the flowers, we'll not talk about them. You seem to have looked at cheap picture postcards a little too much. And this drawing of Tamara doesn't look any more like her than I look like an angel of Botticelli. But all the same, there's something nice about this, and this foreshortening of the arm, that's good, and that upturned foot. Now, don't get crazy ideas into your head! On the whole, your work is not very good. But no matter. You ought to learn to draw. If you studied, I'd be interested in seeing what came out of it."

I looked at him with a certain incomprehension mixed with disgruntlement, for although I hadn't many illusions as to the worth of my drawings, it seemed to me that Max was, all the same, unjustifiably harsh in his judgment. He smiled gently at me.

"You're vexed, aren't you? There's no reason to be, I assure you. It's true that your drawings are bad. How could you be expected to draw well without having learned how to draw? Ninety chances out of a hundred, you'll go on drawing badly, no matter what we do, and maybe I've got unduly excited over some lines that are there by sheer chance. But have a try, anyhow. Register for some classes at the Academy, and work hard. Maybe it will be worth more than to go on tormenting yourself on account of—Tamara. And that's exactly what I want to discuss with you: your relations with Tamara."

I recoiled, instinctively. My relations with Tamara were nobody's business but my own. I didn't want his pity or his help, nor did I want to have him speak to me with familiarity.

"What I'm saying upsets you, my sweet. You think I've not got the right to pry into your affairs. Listen, child. You're too young to save yourself alone. Even I can't manage my own troubles very well. So then . . . But answer me frankly, now. Are you in love with her?"

I did not reply. Was I even sure that I loved Tamara? I knew no one but her, saw no one but her, I had got used to doing not one solitary thing without her. She was indispensable to me. Yes, that was all I could say.

Seemingly, Max was not offended at my silence. After a pause he went on with what he had to say:

"When I first met her, she'd been dragging herself and her sorrows around for I don't know how long, from hotel to hotel, from one love affair to another. At that time she had an extraordinary look. She looked like a half-starved cat, with her eyes dilated to the limit, a wild look that frightened off men. I took her first as a model. The rest followed quite naturally. Then I set her up here. Discreetly. I believed—yes, I believed that a little comfort might transform her. In the beginning she was as sweet, as gentle and loving, as a kitten pulled out of the cistern where it has just missed drowning, a kitten that licks your hand. Yes, that's it. But it didn't last long. Say what you will, there's nothing very loving and gentle about her."

He gave a halfhearted laugh. I realized that he still regretted the time when she had been "so sweet," that it grieved him never to find her so any more, and yet he could not forsake her. At last I understood that he still loved her and that he was unhappy. My feelings of jealousy vanished at once; I forgave him all his bad jokes, his sloppiness, his rather theatrical way of hiding his true simplicity and concealing a hurt that was doubtless greater than mine. Timidly I touched his hand.

"You're very nice, Max," I said, almost happy to feel that Tamara did not treat him any too well. I no longer felt wronged by his presence, and indeed I felt curiously relieved at the thought that Tamara *never* behaved with anyone otherwise than with me, that she did not condescend to love anyone. And although Max was evidently a man, his weakness of character (which I already sensed) placed him in regard to his mistress in a situation similar to mine. Tamara, whom I had believed I would find diminished in stature, recovered all her prestige in my eyes.

Max looked at me kindly. "You're a good child. Try to pull yourself out of this. Oh, I'm not advising you to stop seeing her, I know how hard that is. I do all sorts of things, myself, to have these few evenings with her that she gives me from time to time. I go so far as to treat it as a casual whim, an unimportant affair, just to get her to see me again. Poor Tamara! She has such a horror of love, ever since that idiotic episode . . ."

"Emily?"

"Yes. Oh, so she's talked to you about it? I imagine she was never very tender even before that, but since! All the same . . . All the same, there's you. That's what you want to say? Yes, there's you. Well, she's told me all about your affair, almost from beginning to end, without naming you. It upset me for a minute, even though I was glad for her sake. I thought everything was beginning again, that she was having her revenge, that maybe she was going to be happy. But it didn't work out that way. She will never forgive you for not *being* Emily. If you tried to resist her in no matter what, she would think she was living over again what happened with the other one. Fundamentally, she's suffered more from her defeat than from having lost that girl. And if you give in, she will still not be grateful, since you're *not* that other person. It's not that she's mean, but you must understand her. You see, Tamara is a primitive, in spite of all appearances. She feels a kind of vague tenderness for people she's slept with, and this tenderness lasts as long as her pleasure does. Well yes, she is a little mean, she has the simple cruelty of a barbarian. What makes her dangerous is that she has never been able to get rid of her respect for lying and hypocrisy, those exterior forms of our sentimental refinements. She thinks of them as something enviable, on a par with knowing how to read or write. So she plays with them, affects all kinds of complications, in order to conquer a deeply rooted inferiority complex. I sound like an American psychoanalyst, don't I? But that's it all right. The entire affair with Emily increased her feeling of inferiority to a frightful degree. That's why I want to help you. Never will you pull yourself out of this, all alone . . ."

"What do you mean, help? Help me to do what?"

"To begin with, you must have another interest in your life, something to think about besides her. Urge your father to let you study art at the Academy. Work hard there, and maybe you'll have something to hang on to if she ever hurts you too much. Then, you never can tell, maybe you'll turn out to be somebody."

I tried to thank him, but he cut me short.

"It bothers me to see you acting so spineless, that's all. Now take last night, for instance. You should either have gone back home the minute you saw me, or you should have taken the thing gaily, cracked a few bad jokes, and you should not have come back to the apartment after the movies but should have left us alone. After all, you're not a ninny!"

He patted my cheek affectionately.

"With that said and done," he went on, "I'm now going to dress. Go back home, gather together all your drawings, every one of them, and meet me at three o'clock in Ford's Café, by the harbor. O.K.? Now, take to your heels, if you don't want to see a male human being in all his horror!"

And laughingly he threw the jacket of his pajamas at my head.

Max and I were soon good friends. He made Tamara persuade my father to take me out of school, and Max himself convinced him that my talents were exceptional, overdoing himself on this point, since the main thing was to get permission for me to study at the Academy of Art. With an indulgent shrug my father capitulated to this continued pressure. He considered painting as an amusement about on a par with golf or poker, and often shook his head as he watched me at work, as though I had been making mud pies. But he was good-hearted, he did not want me to be unhappy, and after all, drawing was not a disgraceful occupation for a young girl ripe for marriage. I was bored at Mademoiselle Balde's school, and therefore . . .

Therefore I entered the Academy of Art. It was housed in a big building of modernistic style situated in a steep little street not far from my home. I attended classes there only for a fortnight, since its nail-studded doors closed for the summer vacation on June 20. But this was enough for me to realize that, as Max had predicted, I would need to have courage to learn to draw well. The mocking insolence of my classmates terrified me. The dry lessons in "theory" repelled me. Max knew how to cheer me on and to help me conquer my timidity. When I left the gloomy Academy on June 20, I was full of courage and plans for the coming year.

Then it was that Tamara informed me that she was going to Italy with my father toward the beginning of July. My father had taken no vacation for three years and Tamara loathed staying in Gers during the summer when the town was invaded by tourists of every kind. She made this announcement in such a natural way that I saw there was nothing for me to do but accept it, and, trying for once to follow Max's advice, I pretended to be only slightly annoyed at the idea of spending the summer alone in Gers. My father offered to send me to a summer camp for a few weeks. I refused with horror, my experiences at school and in the art classes having taught me that I did not enjoy being part of a group. He then suggested having my grandfather come to stay with me; at least this would give me a companion at mealtimes. My grandfather replied to the invitation by saying he would gladly accept, on condition that his "nurse," Madame Nina Péroul, accompany him. My father indignantly refused this. So, then, I would remain alone with Julia, who would be feeling as gloomy as I, since the chauffeur was to drive my father and Tamara to Venice.

I resigned myself rather well to the six weeks of solitude, for my father had solemnly authorized me to let Max visit me occasionally "as an instructor in art." The rest of the time I could do what I liked, could draw, could read, and could rest—a thing I rarely had time for and which was much needed. For, no matter what Tamara's mood had been, whether tender, brutal, or mocking, we had indulged in excesses that had left me a little worn out. I told Tamara of these plans in a calmly reasonable way which seemed to interest her.

"So, you don't mind seeing me go away?" she asked, almost ominous at my sovereign calm.

"Darling Tamara," I replied with apparent simplicity, privately blessing Max for his wholesome advice, "I'm terribly sorry not to spend the holidays with you, but since it's inevitable, I'm trying to organize my life in the pleasantest and most profitable way, as far as my work is concerned."

"All the same," she said, after a moment's reflection, "I'm sorry to go off like this without our having a few days to ourselves, in some quiet place."

I made no reply.

"Supposing," she said suddenly, "supposing we spend a week-end at Versaint? I have some friends there who would gladly put us up and aside from them no one else knows me. Don't you think that would be nice?"

I accepted with a joy I carefully dissimulated. Was it this easy to get something out of Tamara? Was it only necessary to seem not to want something to have it? I could scarcely believe it. But there had certainly been a time when, had I asked her to take me to Versaint, she

(161)

would laughingly have refused me that small pleasure.

My father thought it an excellent idea. He was a little worried over leaving me alone for more than a month in the big empty house and would have given me much more than a week-end at Versaint as consolation.

XI

We left on a Saturday morning, taking the slow little local train that crawls up and down the hills of the region. The weather was very fine, all the meadows were full of flowers, and I looked forward to a diverting week-end. We were alone in the train compartment, except for a very respectable and rheumy old gentleman who sat opposite, peering at us over his newspaper, his eyes inflamed as much with indignation as with conjunctivitis. At the end of a half-hour of this observation—Tamara had one arm around me and was always either offering me a bonbon or a magazine, talking the while in an exaggeratedly languid voice—he left the compartment abruptly, his dignity outraged, while we burst into laughter. Tamara then kissed me several times, apparently unable to help herself. All was well.

The afternoon at Versaint was agitated but amusing. We bathed and sunned ourselves on a tiny beach that was crowded with tourists of every nationality, we saw two collections of the latest fashions, a new thing for me, and Tamara bought two traveling costumes without seeming to worry over their price. Toward evening we spent a few "poetic" moments on the cliff overlooking the lake, and at last we went to the house of Tamara's friends, where we were to dine and spend the night. They lived in a dreadful new apartment building in the industrial part of the town.

Tamara's friends were a young couple who lived together without benefit of clergy and made a visible effort to act and look like artists. The woman worked in a store on the main square, where she sold souvenirs and supposed antiques—"and occasionally herself," said the young man cynically, adding, "I make no bones about it, you might as well turn a good thing to some account." In reality, he made frightful scenes of jealousy every night. His own occupation seemed to be trying to get some books of his published, gigantic works eight hundred pages in length, which were "not exactly novels and not exactly poetry."

The dining room was small and low-ceilinged, lit by electricity that had been installed in very ugly candelabras.

"Aren't they hideous?" said the young writer ecstatically. "I adore everything that is twisted, grotesque, baroque! Oh, how wonderful gargoyles are, how wonderful the Middle Ages!"

He himself looked like a gargoyle, with his long nose, his pale face, a lock of hair sweeping his forehead, his mouth twisted up hideously.

"A friend of mine composes music in that genre," the young man went on, as he offered us some thin slices of salami. "I think we're going to collaborate on an oratorio. He's already written some passages that I must say are powerful. And of a very accented, very modern rhythm. . . ."

The main dish was now served: a macédoine of vegetables with slices of cold beef. The abundance of potatoes scarcely made up for the extreme thinness of the slices of meat, which were even finer than the salami had been. Tamara helped herself to wine at regular intervals, and seemed determined to eat nothing.

While the young man talked, his companion listened composedly, all the time watching out of the corner of her eye the dish of potatoes, of which I did not dare take a second helping. I therefore contented myself with a leaf of lettuce, chewing it sadly, while listening in some horror to what the young man said. It was certainly very different from the way art was discussed in the salons of Gers, which was idiotic enough in its own way. But I was used to hearing old gentlemen—ex-statesmen and industrialists—expound their liking for mediocre and outmoded works. I had accepted their pronouncements in youthful bewilderment. Only a few of the more daring old gentlemen expressed a liking for Fauré, Debussy, and Ravel. Some of them dabbled in art, playing sonatas of their own composition or, on their vacations, sketching nice little landscapes, or sometimes composing sonnets to a problematical Beloved.

I was accustomed to that kind of thing, and also to Max's pronouncements, which, I realized, despite my fondness for him, were largely conventional affectations. Because of his talent, you could forgive him for looking and acting like an undergraduate at large; the pose was, you soon learned, only fooling, childish, and rather touching. I always listened indulgently to Max's divagations on art. But never had I thought it possible for a normal and civilized human being to propound such ideas as did this young "writer"—fortunately a sly smile from Tamara reassured me as to their importance.

Tirelessly he talked about himself and his accomplishments. At present he was talking with much gesturing about a scenario he had "written," composed of photographs in which all the best people of Versaint figured recognizably. For a moment I was dazzled at such daring.

"You don't mean to say you actually photographed those people?"

He stared at me contemptuously.

"Oh, that would be too easy! No, my system is allusive, I employ symbols. Do you understand what I mean?"

No, I did not understand. He went to get the photographs to show us while the woman placed at the far end of the table some apples, nuts, and a small plate of cream cheeses. I examined the photographs. It was hard for me to see how views of the most fashionable avenue of Versaint, a grocery store, a dressmaker's mannequin, a kind of upside-down whirlpool, a loaf of bread on a table, and so forth, could concern specific and respectable citizens of Versaint. But since he affirmed that they did, I felt I had no right to argue and confined myself to looking at the pictures rather stupidly.

"Then I get someone who does not have the least idea about what I am doing to write the captions for me! You'll admit that's original, won't you?" said the young man delightedly. And as I continued to look in perplexity at the photographs in my hand, he added, "You know, you ought to look at them upside down, like moving-picture films, it's more synthetic."

The roar of laughter with which he emphasized this remark made him look more than ever like a gargoyle. Obviously, he was determined to convince us that he was a great wit.

While I had been looking at the photographs, the cheese had disappeared.

"Come, let's have our coffee, Simone," said he, and moved to a chair beside the fireplace, which harbored several imitation logs of asbestos—I supposed gas flames issued from them in cold weather.

"Aren't those fake logs awful?" he remarked enthusiastically. "They're just the kind all old maids always have!"

"Awful?" said Tamara suddenly, with inappropriate energy. "They're terrible!"

The young man made a face and Tamara again smiled almost inperceptibly. Simone chose this moment to announce despairingly that they were out of coffee. To compensate for this lack, the writer promised Tamara he would send her a copy of his novel-poem. "It's a completely new kind of writing," said he. "The choruses are realistic, almost colloquial, while the main line of the narrative is poetic, mystic, translucid, as if coming from the beyond, and the voice of the commentator—my own— is savage, pure, moving . . . By the way, I happen to be giving a reading tonight, just for a few friends. Are you by any chance free to join us?"

To my great relief, Tamara replied that we were not.

I did not feel I could stand another quarter of an hour of this young man with the gargoyle head.

"Then you will excuse us," the young man said. "We're in a hurry, they're waiting for us. Simone will show you to your room. We're rather cramped here, so we've only been able to give you one room. But the bed is enormous. We inherited it from a grandfather in the country. It's a real marriage bed."

Tamara began to laugh, and the gargoyle joined in, his mouth twisted with malice.

"By the way, Tamara," he remarked, "I suppose you've initiated this damsel—" He lowered his voice and I could not hear the rest of the sentence.

"Oh, it's impossible to hide anything from you, Jean-Jacques," she said, to my great distress. And she went on, "But she has a very important and respected father."

"I'll keep mum, no fear! Simone, take charge of these ladies."

Simone, who had been tranquilly picking her teeth with a hairpin all this time, opened the door leading into a small corridor, along which she preceded us, while the gargoyle yelped in a transport of delight, "Behold, I am equal to great Sappho!"

It was all I could do to smile at this elegant joke, and I was astonished that Tamara made no objections, for she always said she couldn't stand certain kinds of doubtful pleasantries. Tamara's hand was on the nape of my neck, and it was disagreeable to feel that by this gesture she claimed me as her property.

The room was nondescript, like any third-class hotel

bedroom, with dingy windowshades, a big wooden bed, a crocheted coverlet, and a rather ugly rustic cupboard. At the end of the room a door led into the bathroom, where some laundry was hung up to dry.

"Well, now, I'll leave you," said the young woman. "You'll find some towels in the cupboard, to the right. Be careful, don't knock down all the things in there."

The writer was calling from the corridor, "Are you coming, Simone? Do you expect them to wait all night for us?"

"I'm coming! Excuse me, you two. They're waiting for us, you know. By the way, we may not be awake yet when you get up tomorrow morning. You'll find some bread and honey in the kitchen cupboard."

Not waiting for a reply, she ran out, and shortly afterward we heard the banging of a door.

"Oof! They're gone at last! I'm going to change my clothes before we go out," said Tamara, putting her small leather suitcase on the bed.

"Are we really going out? I thought you said that just to get out of going with them."

"Do you want to spend the entire evening in this horrible room? I didn't come all the way here just for that!"

She went into the bathroom. The shopping that afternoon on top of the swimming had made me tired, and several times during dinner I had had a hard time keeping my eyes open. But I made no objections. It wasn't worthwhile arguing with Tamara over such little things. So I took a clean shirtwaist out of my valise and, as I changed, asked Tamara about her friends.

"Tamara, is that man very intelligent?"

"Jean-Jacques? He's a complete idiot!"

"Oh!" I felt relieved of a great weight. "Is he poor?"

"No, not very. She, poor thing, earns some money."

I was always irritated at the way Tamara referred to other women as "poor thing" or "that person."

"Then he's stingy?"

"Very."

I regretted having refrained, out of decency, from taking a second helping of potatoes.

"I feel a little hungry, still," I said pensively.

Tamara came back into the bedroom. She was wearing her gray flannel slacks and one of her men's shirts.

"My poor darling!" she exclaimed. "Of course you're dying of hunger! Didn't you notice that I didn't eat a thing? We'll have a sandwich and a drink somewhere."

I looked at her in astonishment.

"Surely you're not going out like that?"

"Oh, no?" Her voice was flat and cold as it always was on her bad days. I said nothing more.

"Are you ready?" she went on more gently.

"Yes."

"Come, then. Let's go down."

We took the elevator in silence. The idea of being seen in such an elegant town, accompanied by Tamara rigged out like that, put me to the torture. What if my father heard about it? If he weren't completely oblivious to everything, but instead suspected something of our relations, then what would he think? I kept my fears to myself. Knowing Tamara as I did, I was sure that had I told

(170)

her of them she would have outraged me still more by striking even more compromising attitudes.

Fortunately, people did not look at us very much. Apparently they thought Tamara was simply returning from the beach rather late. I would have liked to tarry in front of the lighted store windows filled with useless and brilliant little things such as one never saw in Gers, or before the big cinemas with their alluring signs, or the café terraces ornamented with round little trees. Some of the terraces were filled with smart-looking crowds, on others orchestras played tangos and sambas, the players in soiled but tinseled uniforms and evidently hailing from countries of the South. But Tamara walked on with quick, determined strides, and I had to follow after. I was beginning to feel tired—we had been climbing up and down the brightly lit streets for some time—when I realized that we had reached a quieter part of town, unmistakably the section where hotel rooms could be had by the day or hour, and where abounded the filthy little bars that always seem to flourish in the neighborhood of railway stations.

Finally, as we turned a corner, we entered a narrow alley, silent and gloomy, a veritable place for holdups, at the end of which could be seen a red neon sign, like a signature, above a low door: "Lucy's Bar." Tamara went toward it with a resolute step.

Through the half-open door could be seen a flight of steps leading down to a small lobby and cloakroom, where the attendant, an old woman of quite decent aspect, seemed to be considerably bored. The muffled sounds of an orchestra could be heard from within. I hesitated.

"Go on in," said Tamara. "There's nothing to be afraid of, you'll not meet your father here."

The cloakroom attendant stood up as she saw us on the steps.

"Well, well!" she said. "It's you, Madame! We haven't seen you for a long time! I suppose you don't live in Versaint any more?"

I had not known that Tamara had ever lived in Versaint. Why had she hidden the fact from me? When she had suggested the week-end, she had acted as though she had never even visited the town.

"I moved away," Tamara replied briefly as she handed over her suède jacket to the old woman.

"Well, I can tell you we've missed you, Madame," said the cloakroom attendant, poking about in her box of numbered discs. "Why, only yesterday Mademoiselle Puck was saying that you hadn't been seen here for a long while. And anyone who knows her knows she doesn't miss just anybody. Oh, no! I don't believe she's come in yet, but she'll surely be here by ten o'clock."

Tamara silently placed some coins on the table and, pushing aside a heavy velvet curtain, introduced me into the smoke-filled room that was Lucy's Bar.

From what I could see of it at first glance, it was a very large basement room, aired by a ventilator giving upon the street. Four huge spotlights at each corner of the room were turned on the round, roped-off dance floor, where moved a compact throng. It made me think of a circus.

(172)

Against the red-painted wall and around this dance floor were arranged several ranks of brown benches and long tables, where a great number of women were standing, sitting, chattering, singing loudly, or calling out to a waiter. I was thunderstruck by the scene, I would have liked to run away or sink into the ground. But Tamara held me firmly by the shoulder and firmly led me between the benches to an unoccupied table not far from the dance floor. Shrill cries sounded from all the tables, some calling out to Tamara. A hand tugged at my skirt, while a hoarse voice said to me, "Don't you want to come over here for a minute, baby?"

Tamara, not seeming at all embarrassed, tranquilly pushed through the crowd, merely laughing and shrugging. At last we reached the small empty table, and I let myself fall on a seat beside Tamara. I had no heart for this adventure. The place frightened me. I was hungry and sleepy, too. Tamara, on the other hand, seemed to be completely at ease.

"Did you notice the cloakroom woman? That old fool used to work in a swank Paris night club, and then I saw her again here. Isn't that funny? And she still talks like she used to at the swank place. Did you notice? 'We've missed you, Madame,' and 'Mademoiselle Puck'! Puck's one of the hostesses here, I used to know her. Not a bad-looking girl, a redhead—not like you, but a redder red. Picturesque place, isn't it? I believe this is the only night club for women in town. Waiter!"

The waiter came up. He was an unattractive and dirty little man who reminded me slightly of Howard.

(173)

"Well, well!" said he. "So you're back! Things still all right with you?"

So everyone knew her! Why had she never talked to me about this place?

"Pretty good, thank you. Bring me one double gin and a ham sandwich. What about you, Hélène?"

"I'll have the same," I stammered, without thinking, upset at being called by my name in such a place.

The waiter left us. But apparently I would have to wait an appreciable length of time for my sandwich, since he was now engaged in changing the color of the spotlights so that the room was plunged in a reddish twilight, suitable to the languorous rhythm of a tango. Near us, a strange pair of women were disporting themselves. One of them, a fat, flushed-faced and thick-necked brunette, dressed in a leather jacket and mechanic's blue overalls, was being passionately embraced by a thin creature who looked something like a cleverly painted and powdered mummy, wearing a flower-printed dress. From time to time the painted mummy uttered words of endearment in a kind of moan. "Baby," said she, "there's just nothing I wouldn't do for you! Ask me to do any crazy thing and I'll do it!"

I watched them contemptuously, but Tamara's eyes held a curious look as she observed these lamentable goings-on. All at once she drew me toward her, tilted up my face, and crushed her mouth against mine. With an immense humiliation and an irrepressible desire to weep, I submitted to this kiss.

"Bravo!" shrieked the mummy. "Encore! Encore!" And

(174)

at the table behind us, an ironic voice counted the seconds slowly: "One . . . two . . . three . . . four . . ."

At last Tamara yielded to my discreet efforts to break away, just as the voice said, ". . . thirty-five! Almost a record!" I dared not look behind me.

"Aren't you having fun?" Tamara asked me with an air of innocence. "You're a little nervous. But it'll wear off, you'll see. Oh, here's our order! Emile! Over here, Emile!"

The waiter approached. "Here I am. That's right, two American gin specials, for you."

"The price will be special too, doubtless," Tamara said with a laugh.

"Oh, as for that . . ." He shrugged. "Doudou has just come in. She's going to sing later on. I'll ask her to sing your song," he said and left.

"What song is your song, Tam?" I asked.

"You'll find out soon. Come, let's dance. You like to dance, don't you? That will put you at your ease."

Without listening to my feeble protest, she pushed me toward the crowded dance floor.

The band, sheltered in a kind of niche contrived of boards nailed against the wall, which apparently communicated with a backstage room, was comprised of four instruments: piano, accordion, guitar, and trumpet. The musicians were big red-faced, sweating, and peaceable-looking men, who would have looked more at home at a village wedding, marching with beribboned instruments at the head of the procession.

For fear of bumping into someone, I pressed myself

(175)

close to Tamara, resting my face against her protective shoulder. She danced well, leading me very adroitly, making me turn and bend as she liked, weak and abandoned in her strong arms, and I felt she liked that. Her lips were tightly set, and on her face there was a faint reflection of that singular beauty she had at the apex of sensual ecstasy. After a moment I dared to look around me, staring, not without anxiety, at the other women dancers. Some of them were stout, straight-haired, placid-looking, and it was hard to determine their sex; there were also some slender young women who glanced over the crowd with a combative look as they drew along with them a peroxided and frizzy-haired partner. Two women near the edge of the dance floor were squabbling over a gay little brunette that each wanted to tear from the arms of her indignant lady partner. It became a fight, with hair pulled and slaps exchanged. A waiter sprang toward them, calling out facetiously, "Ladies! Ladies! Don't interrupt the dance, let the others dance! If you go on like this you'll get thrown out!"

Calm was restored at last. I had involuntarily flinched and Tamara had guessed my fear, for she hugged me tighter. "Don't be afraid, my darling, it's over now," she said smoothly. I realized the satisfaction she was getting out of having her little revenge on me for my independent attitude of the past few weeks.

The women, who had allowed themselves to be separated without too much resistance, hurled at each other one last injury. I almost laughed at their disdainful attitudes. They were swaggering like little fighting cocks.

It was very hot. Everyone's face was streaming with sweat. All at once the pianist stopped and clapped his hands for silence. "Please return to your tables! In a few minutes the floor show will begin. First of all, we have with us the celebrated colored singer—Doudou!" He accompanied these words with a short running scale. We crowded back to our table, and the singer appeared.

Had she been dressed in a cotton print dress, with a bandana twisted round her head, Doudou would have agreeably recalled the fat, faithful, and inexhaustibly indulgent "mammy" of exotic romances. But the celebrated Doudou was sheathed in a shimmering dress of blue-and-black silk, very unflattering to her big, startled-looking eyes, her compressed curves, and her complexion, which was that of one undisputably free of any admixture of white blood.

"Ladies and gentlemen—if there *are* any here," she began in a throaty voice, rolling her *r*'s, "I am going to begin by singing one of our friend Vandreau's songs"— she waved toward the pianist—"*Dans la savane.*"

With this, she began to sing, while making a tour of the floor, stopping from time to time at the tables. As she sang, she made a sort of automatic movement supposedly expressing languor, and rolled her eyes so that suddenly all you could see of them were two bluish-white globes. Her voice was very low, not quite in tune, and remarkably devoid of expression.

"Do you know why she stops ever so often?" asked Tamara, a little before the Negress reached our table. "She's asking people to applaud. Listen: *'Dans ma sava-*

a-a-ne, applaud, please, *la carava-a-a-ne,* applaud, please.' "

"Why?"

"Because they've threatened to fire her. She's no longer young, she's not very popular. Listen. How funny it is . . ."

The Negress had indeed stopped in front of our table, and in a pause of the music she whispered rapidly, "Applaud, please."

"No, it's not funny at all, it's horrible and it's sad!" I said, and there were tears in my eyes as I saw her repeat the performance at the next table. Tamara burst out laughing.

"Horrible! That's so . . ."

She had drunk her glass of gin at a gulp and had sipped a little of mine. Slightly sleepy, I smoked a cigarette, trying not to let it make me cough, and rested my head on her shoulder. Here and there ironic handclapping could be heard. After one more exotic song, which likewise dealt with forests, fragrant winds, and pet parakeets, the Negress announced that she would end with a requested number, the favorite of an old friend of hers. The word "friend" made me jump. The song was *"L'accordéon."* And she began:

> *"Je me souviens d'un air d'accordéon . . .*
> *Un air perdu, une vieille rengaine . . ."*

Tamara looked at me defiantly. And suddenly I wanted to be far away, alone in the night, to be able, undisturbed, to weep out my rage and grief. We had heard that song one day on the phonograph at Ford's Café, and Tamara had declared, in an apparent impulse of tenderness, that she wanted to buy the record as a souvenir of that peaceful afternoon. I had often recalled the sentimental incident at times when I doubted her affection for me, and had always been reassured by its artlessness. But now I realized that she had known this song long before meeting me. I was shorn, all of a sudden, of one of my fondest memories.

The Negress retired in the midst of excessive applause and of ironic demands for more. Several women shouted *"Bis, bis!"* in a roar of laughter. Doudou, impassive, bowed several times without seeming to notice anything out of the way, then retired definitely in the midst of thunderous applause and shouts that were very like jeers.

The band announced a quarter of an hour of uninterrupted dancing before the second part of the floor show. Again the dance floor filled up. A woman paused near our table, continuing a conversation she had begun elsewhere, while Tamara tried to kiss me. I resisted as best I could, wounded by her deliberate malice in letting "her song" be sung. She could at least have found a pretext of some kind to ask that it *not* be sung! But she had wanted to hurt me, she had wanted to show me that I was not as detached from her as I pretended to be.

The woman went on with her conversation, not caring at all that she could be overheard: "And it seems nowadays us women can't wear pants any more without people calling us Dykes!"

In stepping back, she bumped into our table. Turning round, she exclaimed, "Tam! So that's where you are.

They told me you'd come. Ha, it's easy to see you're having a good time! Can I sit down?"

Without waiting for a reply, she seized a chair and sat down facing us, her elbows on the table.

"Hey there, Emile! Bring me a vermifuge or something!" she called out, in the midst of general laughter. Then, speaking lower, "What're you drinking? Gin? You ought to know there's nothing fit to drink in this place but lemonade. All the rest is faked, or methylated spirits. I was sick as a dog with dysentery three months ago from drinking their slop!"

Very ill at ease, I was doing what I could to wipe off some lipstick traces Tamara had left on my cheek.

"There's more on the left side of your mouth," the strange woman said, observing me. She was tall, with a bushy head of very red hair, yellow eyes, a turned-up nose, and the face of an adolescent boy.

"So, you're hooked up with this baby?" she asked Tamara, who sat there with a dazed look in her eyes, a cigarette dangling at the corner of her mouth. She had been drinking gin again, and from her whole aspect you would have said she and Puck were two of a kind.

"Oh, for a little while," said Tamara, beginning to laugh.

"Will you dance this number with me, Mademoiselle?"

The question was asked by the fat woman in the leather jacket whom I had noticed earlier. She was standing in front of me and bowing ceremoniously.

"Nothing doing," said the redhead. "I've retained her for the whole evening."

The fat woman went off without insisting.

"She's a wild one," said Puck confidentially. "Once she gets hold of you there's no getting away. You've heard about her, Tam. She's the one that did three years in the clink for beating up Lilli . . ."

I yawned, involuntarily.

"Here, come and dance, baby! I'll wake you up a little. All right with you, Tam? I'll bring her back in good condition."

All this colloquy transpired without anyone's thinking of consulting me. Surely, I thought, Tamara would not allow this, surely she would not oblige me to go off with this unknown creature, of whom I was afraid? And supposing she abandoned me here in this frightful place! Tamara only looked at me mockingly. She guessed my fright, I know now, and it amused her. She was remembering my emancipated attitudes when I had entered the Academy, and when I had announced to her the decisions I had made with Max, as though she were in no way concerned, and how calmly I had heard of her proposed trip to Italy. She had been insulted by all that and was now trying to make me regret it, to remind me that, after all, I was nothing without her but a timid girl, stupid and ignorant, and that she could do anything she liked with me.

"Take her off and keep her as long as you like," she said to Puck with assumed carelessness. "All I ask is that you bring her back before closing time."

Her eyes were still full of mockery as she watched us go toward the dance floor, Puck steering me by the arm, while the women we passed called jeeringly, "Pu-u-uck! Are you afraid someone's going to carry her off?"

Why, oh why had Tamara allowed this? It was like one of those nightmares that never end. Impossible to get loose, to run away, in the midst of this jeering crowd. I forced myself not to think about anything, but just to let myself drift. But Puck would not permit this.

"Can't you talk?" she asked. "You might thank me, all the same! If it hadn't been for me, you'd have got stuck with that fat old fool and there'd have been no way out for you, you'd have had to go home with her."

"Tamara would have done something about that," I murmured in a shaky voice.

"Tam? You don't know her. Just look at her now! If you think she looks jealous, you're easily convinced."

Indeed, Tamara was watching the dancing with an absorbed and ironical expression. I made an effort to hide my suffering and to dance in a free and easy way. My partner noticed this at once and took occasion to draw me closer, pressing her pointed chin down against my forehead, and at each step catching and holding my legs with hers.

"You don't need to be afraid of Tam, baby! She don't give a damn! And I've known her a lot longer than you've known her, please remember."

She said nothing for a while, then began to question me. "You're not used to dives like this, are you?"

"No . . ." I would have preferred not to confess my inexperience, but feared it was all too evident.

"Anyone can see that. Is Tamara the first one?"

I nodded.

"And you've never been with anybody else? You don't want to answer me? That's O.K. I don't mind. You're a good dancer. Do you do everything as well as this?"

At this question I must have flushed considerably, for she began to laugh.

"I'll bet you do! Oh, and I can find out, if I want to. She'll tell me everything, even if it's only to make you mad. You don't want to tell me anything, eh? I see you're well trained. She had one before, did Tam, and she brought her here sometimes. It was the same thing then. That one didn't dare tell me anything. Though she wasn't such a baby as you are. She'd already lived, that one! Afraid of Tam, maybe; she can be a devil. Look at the way she's sopping up that gin again. I bet you'll have some night!"

The band stopped a moment, then went on with a tango. The red-headed creature kept me forcibly there, on the floor.

"You needn't waste time trying to get away. We'll not go back to the table till the next floor show. This is my business; to make the customers dance. If it wasn't you it'd be some of those old American broads over there, do you see them?"

The light turned red, and Puck led me in a very slow tango. It was then that I suddenly realized she was holding me with only one arm while, with her free hand, she was trying to caress my breast. I tried to break away, I was full of shame and near to weeping, but the crowd and Puck's arm holding me tight made it out of the question.

"Come on, be nice to me! She can't see anything and there's too big a crowd. Anyway, she's already tight. And I've told you Tam don't mind! And you like it, don't you?"

Until then I had never experienced shame to this degree; in fact, I had never actually realized that my relations with Tamara could be classed as shameful. I suddenly understood that they were, and at the same time a wave of heat seemed to go over me, it rose between my shoulder-blades, and I felt an indescribable apprehension as well as an unspeakable fascination. Again I tried, but more weakly, to break away from this embrace, to withdraw from this person who now had her hand inside my blouse and was caressing my breasts.

"Don't be afraid. Everybody does this, here," she whispered.

I no longer struggled, but passively let her do what she liked. Only, I repelled her kiss. I don't know why. Maybe it was to preserve at least the memory of Tamara's first kiss, to keep it free from shame, that shame that would now never leave me.

"Come with me," said the woman, after a moment. "I've got a room upstairs. All we have to do is slip past the band, she'll not get wise to a thing."

"Oh, no!" I cried. I could let myself be lulled by the dance, by the glass of alcohol to which I was unaccustomed; I could surrender myself to these caresses on the dance floor—was almost obliged to, because of the crowd. But to go upstairs and remain alone with this unknown woman, in a room I did not know, that was different! Also, supposing Tamara went away and left me? Or supposing she took it into her head to be angry? Supposing she were to tell my father that I behaved badly with her? You could never be sure what she might do.

"So it's 'no,' is it?" Puck said, looking at me contemptuously.

"I'm sorry," I stammered.

"You're sorry, but you're scared of her, you're afraid she'd give you a drubbing. Oh, I understand. Some people have nerve, and some haven't. And when you're scared stiff, that's that, eh, baby?"

She finished the dance in haughty silence, then, with dignity, took me back to Tamara's table.

Tamara had been nervously chain-smoking all this time, and by the fixed stare she gave me I realized that she must have been drinking a lot.

"So, you had a good time?" she said.

"Yes, very," the woman answered for me. "She had such a good time that if I was you I'd take her home right away. She'll end up by getting herself raped."

"You think so?"

"Yes. And you, you look as though you'd been soaking in gin. You'd better go home too. Do you think you can walk?"

"You'll see!"

But Tamara did not seem to want to stand up at all.

"She's in terribly bad shape," said Puck, looking at Tamara with the eye of an expert. "She got any money?"

"Yes, in her purse."

"Fine. Now, you'll pay while I go get a taxi. Emile! The kid's going to pay the bill."

Puck went out at a run. Tamara did not say a word. Her beautiful face was pale and drawn, her dark-ringed eyes were singularly glazed. She looked at the waiter without seeing him, as he stood there in front of her.

"Let's see," he said, "you had four gins, two whiskies, and some sandwiches."

"Two whiskies?" I said, amazed, thinking he was trying to take advantage of Tamara.

"Yes, Mademoiselle. Madame went on drinking while you danced. Surely you don't think two gins would put Madame into this condition! Maybe you can take the money out of her bag? They're calling me . . ."

Tamara did not make a sign as I took her purse out of her pocket and paid the bill. By that time Puck was waving at me from the end of the room.

"The taxi has come, Tamara," I said. "Are you ready?"

I wondered if she would be able to reach the door. However, she got up and walked across the room mechanically but steadily, and reached the cloakroom. I hurried to help her into her jacket, while she stood there, looking vaguely at nothing.

"Goodbye, Puck," she said in a hard voice.

We went toward the door.

"What about my tip?" asked the redhead. "I got the taxi for you, didn't I?"

"Oh, Mademoiselle Puck!" said the old cloakroom attendant, like a grandmother scolding a naughty child.

"Go to hell," said Puck.

"If you keep on like this," said the old woman, "I'll have to report you. Anyway, can't you see? Madame's in no condition to understand a word you say. If the young lady wishes to give you something supplementary I can't prevent you from accepting, naturally . . ."

Puck looked at me insultingly, then burst into a laugh.

"Oh, I won't trouble her! She's already given me something."

The old woman looked at me sadly, and on top of all my worries about how we were to get home, I felt hurt by that reproachful look.

We went out. Fortunately I remembered the address of Tamara's friends, and gave it to the taxi driver. We had come to Lucy's Bar on foot, but I hadn't realized the distance that separated us from our lodgings. However, it seemed to me that the cabby was following a series of little streets that we had not seen on our way down, and they seemed to get narrower and darker all the time. I began to worry. Maybe the cab driver was taking us out into the mountains to murder us, or at least to rob us. We wouldn't be able to go to law about it, for we would then have to tell where we had taken the cab, and then . . .

I glanced at Tamara's face, but it was still a blank; her eyes were staring straight ahead, there was a pinched look about the nose which made her look like a corpse, her lips were tightly closed, and she seemed hardly to be breathing.

"Tamara!"

"What?"

I did not know what to say. I hadn't expected those lips to open, and the sound of the metallic voice that had escaped them had surprised me.

"Do you think we're far from our place?"

"I don't know. If we'd reached there, the driver would have stopped. Leave me alone, Emily. I'm not feeling well."

I hushed, horrified at this calm drunkenness that resembled madness. Why did she call me Emily? To hurt me still more? But there was no trace of mockery in her expression to indicate either defiance or enjoyment at hurting me. Was she under the impression that time had turned back, was she living again several years in the past? In a near-paroxysm of terror, I could imagine myself alone in a deserted field near the inert body of Tamara and completely without money. . . . At this point, I cast a glance outside, and recognized—with what joy!—that we were slowly climbing one of the wide tree-bordered avenues of Versaint, but empty now, and unlighted. Then, a somber front looked familiar: a bank. And there was a street corner I had seen before. Some prostitutes standing there stepped forward into the light as they heard the taxi approach. At last we had gone by the station, and I felt completely reassured. We were not lost. But I had another kind of fear now. Tamara might raise a rumpus in the quiet building. If only she would consent to go noiselessly to our room. . . .

The cab driver was humming a tune to himself, tranquilly, and from time to time talked encouragingly to himself. ("Don't go to sleep, old man! You've still got two or three more runs to make before you've finished your day. . . .")

At last he stopped in front of a building that I recognized. I paid the driver. Tamara got out without hesitation, holding herself very straight. She really did not look drunk, but more as if she were under the influence of some strange madness. All the same, she could not open the door of the apartment and I had to take the key from her.

The apartment was dark and still. Our hosts must not have come in yet, or else they were already asleep. Not finding the electric light switches, we had to feel our way to our room. There, a weak electric bulb that we had left burning faintly lit up the big bed with its crocheted coverlet, the dingy window shades, the hideous rustic cupboard. I could not help feeling a horrible sadness at the sight of that room, at the thought of the evening just passed, and at the contrast all this made with the trip to Versaint as I had imagined it.

Tamara, having thrown her jacket upon a chair, sat down on the bed.

"Come here," she said.

Not without a certain fear, I obeyed.

"Sit down. Now, you're going to answer me. Why did you see that girl again? You know very well I forbade you to. Why did you write to her? I'm sure you wrote to her! Answer me!"

She was holding my wrist, and I remained motionless with horror, staring at her, fascinated by that face which showed she was living in the past—two, three, maybe ten years in the past. I was afraid of her as one is afraid of madmen, and at the same time I wanted to know, I wanted her to speak again, wanted her to reveal more of that past in which I had no part, that past which had risen to the surface of her troubled mind, by I knew not what wild phenomenon. What coincidence had released this strange mechanism? Would I ever know?

But then she took me into her arms, pushed me back on the bed, and gently kissed my face.

"If only you'll tell me the truth, I'll forgive you," she said. "But tell me the truth! Tell me . . ."

Even had I wanted to pronounce a word, even had I found a reply to make, I could not have spoken, so tight was my throat. Quite near mine, I could see her moon-struck face.

"You imagine I don't know anything, that's why you keep still! But you'll end up by saying something, I'll see to it that you do. There! Take that!" And she slapped my face again and again, violently.

I tried to protect myself with my hands, my arms, but she kept on striking, savagely. At last, through my tears, I just managed to say:

"But I'm Hélène, Hélène, Hélène!"

"Hélène . . . Well, what difference does that make? Didn't you dance with her? Didn't you go to walk with her on the terrace? I tell you, I saw you!"

The mean and sly expression on her face was frightful. In the beginning I had suppressed my cries, for fear of causing a scandal, but now I feared for my life and I struggled, trying even to call out for help. Tamara held me by the throat. Then she took off her leather belt and began to lash me with it. At times she recognized me, and intentionally struck me, brutalizing me for being a stranger and an enemy, and for having broken her illusion. At times she sank back into her dream, and spoke to me tenderly. Then again, with fury, she struck me. It went on and on. When in her dream, she murmured sweet and incomprehensible things to me hoarsely, sobbed out reproaches, even implored me:

"I know I did it too, my beloved, but I didn't do it to hurt you. Forgive me, Emily, Emily . . ."

She took my terrified face between her hands, scrutinized it as if to superimpose that other face.

Suddenly she went white, passed a trembling hand over her forehead, and fell back like a dead weight on the pillow. Was she asleep? Had she fainted?

Bruised, trembling in all my limbs, I waited for a long while. She did not move again. At last I undressed noiselessly, and slipped into bed, after turning off the light. This frightful scene had so exhausted me that I sank at once into sleep.

I was the first to wake up. Cautiously, I got out of bed. I staggered. It seemed to me I had not stopped trembling all night. I dressed in the bathroom. Not a sound came from the bedroom and at last I had managed to button my blouse and tie my shoes. I didn't even take time to wash my face, which was swollen with tears. I leaned out of the window to see what time it was by a town clock. It was five o'clock. When had we come back? What time had it been when I went to sleep? I hadn't the least idea.

Going back into the room and holding my breath, I snatched up my little valise and went out. Before closing the door, I dared to cast a glance toward the bed. Flat on her back, completely dressed, her arms back of her head, Tamara seemed still to be sleeping profoundly. Her face, in the early morning light that came through the paper shades, seemed to me singularly aged, naked, fatigued.

In the hall I trembled with fear lest a board squeak and Tamara, woken up, would spring out at me, call me back, question me, oblige me to remain there. But nothing transpired and without mishap I reached the door of the apartment, went out, closed it behind me, and ran down the stairs as fast as I could, but on tiptoe. I dared not take the elevator for fear it would make a noise. At last I was in the street.

The town was still enveloped in the blue mist of a summer morning. On the benches slept one or two beggars, twitching feverishly as people do who are only half asleep and are afraid, even in their sleep, that a policeman may come along. There were no trolley cars; I did not know when the trains left. All the same, I went toward the station, stopping occasionally to breathe in the fresh morning air. Once I stopped a minute to see a curious spectacle. In front of a café that was still closed, some empty kegs of beer were stacked, waiting for a delivery truck to take them away. An old beggar-woman was scraping out the bottoms with a rusty tin can and avidly drinking the few drops she had been able to scoop up. This was also a custom in Gers: every morning ragged old people squabbled in front of the cafés over a few drops of stale beer. I was used to the sight. Even so, that old beggar-woman seemed to be a terrible omen.

At last, near the station, I saw an open café. Some work-men in blue overalls were drinking coffee there, talking in hushed voices as if out of respect for the quiet morning atmosphere. I could sit down there, with them, and wait for my train.

I went in. The proprietor, a big, red-faced man who was reading his newspaper near the cash register, looked at me in surprise. He was probably not used to seeing, at five o'clock in the morning, a young girl come in, carrying a suitcase, and red-eyed from weeping. I caught a glimpse of myself in a looking glass and noted that I had forgotten to comb my hair.

"Your order, please?"

"A cup of coffee, please."

"It's five francs," he said, as he turned his back to pick up a cup.

Suddenly I recalled, with a wave of horror, that I had no money on me. Since I never carried a handbag, I had been afraid of losing the money my father had given me, and had handed it over the day before to Tamara. I had not thought of it until now, in such feverish haste had I been to get away. How could I explain this to that man who was standing there waiting, after having put down before me a smoking hot cup of coffee?

"I—I'm sorry, sir. I've forgotten my money," I mumbled, and I started to leave. But he came out from behind his counter to hold me back.

"And you've just thought of it now?" he asked, looking as though he suspected me of the worst.

"I was hurrying to catch the train."

(193)

"Hurrying, were you? But there's no train before seven o'clock!"

I was speechless before this argument, which seemed to delight him.

"Don't you worry," he said more gently, "I see what's up. You've run away from home, haven't you? Well now, forgetting your money is a sign, do you hear? It's a sign! So, go back home and don't ever do such a thing again! But first, drink up your coffee, all the same. That will make you feel better."

I obeyed him without a word, so worn out and discouraged was I by this last stroke of fate.

"They're bad to you, are they, your parents?" he went on almost paternally. "I understand. They shook you up a little, maybe. But no doubt you deserved it."

I could not keep back a tear.

"Oh, now, now, it's not that bad," he said. "Such things happen to everybody."

He looked at my arm, on which a blow of the belt had left a long bluish trace.

"But now, think: if you went away, they'd soon catch you. And then, where would you go to? You ought to thank God that you forgot your money. Now, hurry back home. Maybe no one's awake there yet. Run along, run along. . . ."

Gently he pushed me toward the door, and I did not struggle. Maybe it was a sign, as he said. His reasoning might not be valid, but other reasons came to my mind. How would I explain this unexpected return to my father? How would Tamara take my flight? Maybe she was already awake, maybe she had already called the police, told her friends. I would probably find the house in an uproar of shouts, there would be reproaches. They would ask me, "Where have you been?" They would say, "Why did you run away? You're crazy!"

And if I did not go back to Tamara, where could I go, and how could I go anywhere without money? As I walked slowly along, carrying my valise, my head down, my whole body still aching with bruises, I did not see the morning, the trees, or the bright empty streets.

When I reached the building, all my courage failed me. I sat down on a bench to wait a minute. My heart throbbed. After a few seconds, an old woman who was wandering on the sidewalk came to sit down beside me, first asking permission, which I granted with the usual polite phrase. I said it mechanically, but as she spread out her dusty and ragged dress, she seemed to want to talk, and to talk about herself. Her words were addressed to me, but she seemed to be just thinking aloud.

"Thank you, you're very polite," she began. "And it's a rare thing, nowadays. Take my grandson, he's twelve years old and he's all the time upsetting garbage cans. I don't like that, it annoys me a lot, because, you see, I'm the one that has to do with garbage cans, and he ought to keep his hands off them . . ."

I bounded up and went toward the house. That kindly café owner! And now, that old madwoman! It was all too awful. I felt I was under a curse. A destiny hung over me which obliged me to go back to Tamara.

I rang the doorbell of the apartment. The gargoyle-headed young man opened the door. He was wearing a sumptuous dressing-gown of orange-colored velvet.

"What in the world! It's you? What got into you to go out at this hour?"

"I took a walk!" I replied rudely, hoping he would stop his questioning at this point.

"But you're carrying your valise!"

I went in and started toward the bedroom without replying. He followed me.

"I understand. You wanted to go away, but you weren't able to! Oh, love, love! See here: we heard a little noise last night, but we did not intervene. We're discreet. . . ."

I still did not reply, and he shrugged and went back to his room.

Tamara was still asleep, in the feeble morning light. I put my valise down. I was cold. There was nothing for it but to sit there on a shaky chair and wait till she woke up.

In her sleep she had crossed her hands on her breast. Beneath her long closed eyelids a violet shadow showed, and a single tear had rolled down her hollow cheek, leaving a trace. For the first time I realized that she was thirty-six years old.

I forgot my anger, I forgot my sadness, so that for a second time I felt nothing but pity for that beautiful face that one night of drunkenness had so ravaged. At the corners of her mouth, those fine wrinkles that bitterness had made had become even deeper, and from time to time a gentle and weary sigh escaped her breast, as though sleep had shorn her of all spitefulness and artifice. I felt the need of total abnegation, almost of atonement. For, though I had the right to blame her a hundred times more than I did, at that moment I confusedly felt a kind of shame, as though in some way my youth, my father's wealth, and my hopes for the future cheated her of something, and so, out of a desire to forget and in the hope of recovering a vestige of the integrity of my feeling for her, which she herself had debased, I took off my shoes and lay down beside her.

I reflected, as I looked at her desolate profile, that we were lying side by side like the recumbent forms on the tombs in cathedrals. Lying there at her side, I almost had the impression that I was protecting her. Without waking her, I gently put my hand on her shoulder.

XII

"So here we are," said Max, closing the door, "alone together for a six weeks' honeymoon."

You could see that, though he jested, his heart was not in it.

We had just seen my father and Tamara drive away in the big black car, which had been furbished up for the occasion. They were going to see Venice, Florence, and Rome. They were loaded down with maps, guidebooks, and luggage—three pigskin trunks, of which two were brand-new ones given by my father to Tamara and marked with her initials. She adored traveling, and for two years, ever since she had lived in Gers, she had had no opportunity to travel. As she said goodbye to us, she was radiant, while my father's face as he looked at her had expressed a ponderous satisfaction that had irritated me. He had taken her by the arm to help her into the car. In doing that, he seemed to proclaim so flagrantly that she belonged to him that Max and I both, simultaneously, shrugged and felt like saying, "We're aware that she is your mistress!"

And away they went.

We had closed the big door behind us. My father had been so preoccupied with thoughts of his journey that this, added to his natural irresponsibility, had not enabled him to realize how imprudent was his conduct in leaving me, a sixteen-year-old girl, alone and free to do what I liked, invite whomsoever I liked. True, we had no relatives with whom he could have left me, and I had energetically refused the idea of going to any of the boarding schools or summer camps he had suggested.

Julia was weeping in the kitchen over the departure of the chauffeur. The office workers were away on their vacation. The house, with its shutters half closed, was plunged in cool semidarkness. Max and I took refuge in my bedroom, both victims of the same melancholy.

"All the same," said Max, summing up our thoughts, "that was something, the way she kissed us goodbye! Did you notice? It was as though we were poor relations, aged aunts in veils, and she wanted to avoid having her cheeks touched with damp lips!"

"It was on account of Papa," I said, without conviction.

"He wasn't there."

"But he might have come up any minute."

"Evidently she was so happy to get away that she couldn't think of anything else. She'd wanted to take a trip for such a long time. It was only natural."

Max was the one, now, who was thinking up excuses for her. Oh, yes, he loved her more than I did.

Halfheartedly, he tried to talk about something else, no matter what.

"Supposing you tell me a little about that damned art school. What did they teach you in the fortnight you went there?"

"Do you really want to talk about art?"

"No, of course I don't."

We were both thinking about Tamara. I could not keep back my thoughts and said in a low voice, "She is in the car now, and you may be sure she's not thinking any more about us than if we had never existed. She's putting on the affectionate-little-woman act now, for Papa, who will be entranced."

"Do you hold it against her?"

"Wouldn't you, if you were in my place? I'm a mass of bruises!"

"Oh, that's not the worst. She's like that. One day she loves you, she's sweet, good, charming. Next day she kicks you out. Then, three days afterward, if you go back, she welcomes you as if nothing had happened. What did she say to you about the Versaint affair?"

"Nothing. She seemed to have forgotten everything."

"And of course you were so glad to have her sweet and calm again that you didn't even dare to mention it! Do you know what we ought to do? How do you intend to spend the vacation?"

"Why, drawing, reading. Unfortunately it's going to be horribly hot. And so many tourists come here. Six weeks—that's a long time."

"And it may be longer," he said bitterly. "When I asked her how long she expected to be away, she said, 'Theoretically, six weeks, but it depends on the weather and on René.' She's capable of dragging him God knows where, and God only knows when we'll see them again!"

"What did you start to say just now, about what we

(200)

ought to do?" I said this chiefly in an effort to change the subject, for he seemed to be really full of grief.

Max was half reclining on my bed, meditating.

"As for me," he said, "I'm going to the country for a time. I'll be frightfully blue, I'll not see anyone, I'll work. The songs of despair are the most beautiful ones, as everyone knows."

"Where in the country?"

"My place. Ten kilometers away. The only people there are a venerable old man who takes care of some pink and charming pigs, a young shepherd who leads out to pasture two skinny cows—my entire property—and a charming lady of sixty-four summers who cooks my soup for me. Not very gay, you'll admit. But it's cooler there than here, and I'll have tranquillity for my work. You know what? You ought to pack up and come along with me on my old motorcycle, you, me, and our painting kits. We will discourse on love, we will paint nothing but orchards, and we might even sleep together. What do you say to that?"

I looked at him in horror.

"Max, you're not being serious?"

"What? About us sleeping together? Why, at your age, my sweet, Arab girls already have three or four children! Please note that if this program doesn't please you, we can adopt another as easily. You could take the old lady, I could take the young shepherd, and we could then project upon our canvases the greenish light of perverse loves. But I can't see why you repulse the offer of my favors, having penetrated my radiant intimacy at our very first encounter."

"No matter what, it's impossible. My father would find out. And then, it wouldn't be quite decent. Remember, Max, you're Tamara's lover!"

"Hmm . . . There's some remembering you might do yourself, my pretty one. However, I don't insist. If you don't want to, you don't want to. I'm not going to rape you. All the same, you ought to come to the country, if only as a friend. We can play with the little pigs, we can go to the mountain to pick flowers."

This easygoing and cynical way of considering the possibility of relations between us struck me with amazement. Despite everything, I still held certain illusions, notably that for a young girl to take a lover was an inconceivable and terrible thing.

"Max, tell me. Do you *want* to sleep with me?"

My curiosity was augmented by the ever new delight I took in using the cynical and crude vocabulary of "grownups." Max looked at me benevolently.

"It would not be unpleasant. You're a pretty little thing."

I blushed slightly, in spite of myself, and then reddened still more at the very thought of blushing.

"And me, I think you're very nice. But I really don't believe I want to . . ."

"Oh well, nothing's going to force you to it, my pet."

He took out his pocket mirror and contemplated his face with outrageous satisfaction and many grimaces.

"Queer, though: I'm a good-looking young man, with intelligent eyes, romantic curls, a robust torso. I don't see what you have against my seductive personality."

"It's just that you're a man. I'm not used to a man."

He began to laugh.

"You'll get used, quick enough. And with me, just think, once tried, always used, as they say in the advertisements."

"That's just it. It's the first step that counts!" I said, laughing, too.

He slid carelessly to the bottom of the bed and sat beside me.

"We could always have a try. Kiss me."

Why not? This was what I at once said to myself. It would be as good a way as any to be finished with Tamara. All week long I had reproached myself for my own cowardice, for that physical desire for her that never left me, even in the midst of anger. If only I could desire or love someone else, it would be so much simpler. I looked at Max, his mischievous eyes, his big healthy mouth showing all its white teeth in a smile, and leaning toward him I awkwardly pressed my lips to his. But the minute he began to kiss me, I fought him off savagely, bursting into tears. Repulsed, he looked at me stupefied.

"I can't," I sobbed. "It's not my fault, Max, I just can't."

Fearing that I had annoyed him, as soon as I had recovered my calm, I drew near him once more, a little ashamed of myself. But almost paternally he laid my head against his man's shoulder.

"Oh, the bitch!" he murmured angrily. "What has she done to us!"

Even so, I might have gone to the country with Max had I not, barely a week after Tamara's departure, fallen a little ill. For two days I endured frightful headaches, which I attributed to the hot weather. Julia was not very sympathetic. Ever since I had made Tamara's acquaintance I had gradually stopped caring for Julia with the childish love which had formerly flattered her; I no longer went to sit with her in the kitchen beside the stove, while she knitted. She therefore considered herself as discharged of my care, and treated me affectionately as a "big girl," which I did not even notice. All the same, on the third day, when I complained of a severe sore throat, and of a fever which constantly became worse, she summoned Max, who was staying for a few days at the Rempart des Béguines, and whom my father had innocently designated as the person to call upon in case of disaster.

Max looked at me with a competent air and declared, "You're obviously going into a decline, it's an illness from which a girl cousin of mine died." But nevertheless he called the doctor: I had scarlet fever. . . .

Next day I was covered with red spots, I was delirious, and I no longer knew what was going on about me. First of all, it was the ceiling that rose and fell, rising very high, making little waves. I was in a boat, I was gradually drowning in white waves perfumed with lavender and marked with my initials. Quicker, quicker. . . . I had only a shred of consciousness left, a long colored thread which held up my head on the surface of the waves, preventing me from disappearing completely in that torpor which was near but always just eluded me. At the cost of infinite effort, I managed to lower my head a little to catch some cloth between my teeth. If only I could bring it up to my eyes, then all that burning pain in them would stop. But around me there were no more cool waves. It was sand that I touched with my dry and feverish hands. Sand. I counted each grain. Either it was sand or it was snow. I knew that snow could be burning, too. I had fallen into the snow, I was lost in a waste of snow. Why? Because I was unhappy. "I'm unhappy . . ." These words resounded as though they came from the depths of a marine grotto. Could it be the sea? In any case, I had heard, "I'm unhappy." Or maybe it was, "Is she unhappy?"

Someone was taking care of me. I drank at last, thirstily. But where was the glass? I lightly bit its smooth and shining surface, polished like a piece of ice, but I tried in vain to touch it with my hands. My arms went out on all sides, like the arms of a windmill. Then came tranquillity. And I saw that I was lying in the former bedroom of my mother, after I had studied for some time, without recognizing them, the blue-and-white curtains that she had loved. They were very restful, those curtains. They almost banished the pain in my head.

Why did they leave me alone? I was ill. They ought not to leave me alone.

"Julia!" I cried out.

Someone got out of an armchair: it was Max. Why was he there? He was supposed to have gone to the country.

"Julia!"

The door opened, on a great blackness. It was not Julia. It was Tamara who came in.

"Make me well, Tamara! All you have to do is put one of your cool hands on my head and the pain will go, I will be well again, or I'll die, I don't care which."

But she only applied to my temples some small, shining and pointed instruments. Oh, this was too much! She had found still another means of tormenting me. . . . Yes, she pressed them against my temples with all her might, the pain increased tenfold, she wanted to kill me now because she hadn't succeeded in killing me in Versaint.

"No, no, Tamara!" I screamed. And she replied in a loud voice, "Cover yourself up better!" She was trying to make me die of heat, to smother me. . . .

Then all of a sudden everything was over, and she was coming down a blue path from the curtains to me, carrying a bunch of white carnations. She held them out to me with a smile. Was she going to kiss me? Her face grew bigger, it looked like a cat's face, she licked her lips with a violet-colored tongue. Oh, kiss me, kiss me, bite my lips gently, come near me, dearest Tamara, so cool, brown and smooth, like a brook. There she was, with that bunch of white flowers, like a pillow, her face leaning down over me, closer, closer, smothering me. . . .

"Enough, enough, go away, I don't want this!" I cried. The flowers pressed against my face, wet flowers, smelling of ether or vinegar. Her eyes were there again, like pomegranates burst open, with milk and blood and the sap of trees flowing from them. One drop of the blood, one tear only fell on me. She was crying about me. I was dead. I would never again see anything but the inside of my eyelids, gold streaked with red. Gold, probably because a lamp had been placed near my corpse. But where was that lamp? I turned my head: there was the wall, and a mirror. The lamp was in the depths of that mirror, at the end of a very long corridor of polished mahogany. If only I could reach it I would be saved. Lamps are placed beside dead people, but living people pick up the lamps, put them out, light them . . .

I must have been talking out loud, for now there was Julia, going toward that mahogany door. I called out to her, "The lamp, Julia!" But she did not understand a thing, she was too stupid. And I called again, "Julia!" There was no more light. It was the dark night of a tomb. "Cold tomblike night . . ." I said, and I could laugh about it. For they'd made a mistake on that score! It was not cold in the tomb, but hot and damp. A feeble light filtered through the curtains, through the network of the little paths of the curtains that lighted up like a stage setting. Something was happening there, that was sure. I stared absorbedly at the white paths and the blue paths. I stared so hard that I perceived some red-and-brown spots. Mushrooms, perhaps. I forgot that I was dead. My eyes left me, sank into the great, the immense curtain of paths, as if into soft mud, and remained there until a black, hairy disk intervened. I wanted to brush it away, and my fingers got caught in a mass of curls, a forest of curls . . .

"They have their nerve, these sick people!" someone said, and I recognized Max's voice. He had come to save me, to keep Tamara from burying me alive. Quick, quick, I thought, he must act quickly while I was not yet dead. I must explain what he was to do quickly, before he went away. I called out:

"Tamara . . ."

I heard Max's reply from a distance. But why did he turn his back to me? I couldn't see his face. Strain my eyes as I would, all I could see was long curly hair, which grew longer, longer. But his voice was the same, I managed to hear it.

"She's coming, my child, she's coming."

Oh heavens, he thought I was asking for her! No, no, she must be kept from coming! For she wanted to get rid of me. . . .

And now he had gone. I felt I must shout to him, shout loudly. But he had disappeared. They all managed to disappear. But there were no doors. They went out through the mirror, through that immense stairway at the end of the mirror, a stairway going up in a spiral. It made me dizzy, the stairway turned with me. Then I could see nothing. And I cried out, "Wait for me! Max! Tamara!" And I was falling, falling, into the depths of the sea for which I had so longed. . . .

In the pinkish yellow light of the Chinese lampshade, Tamara goes to and fro in her Persian dressing-gown. I am dreaming. For the first time I am dreaming tranquilly. All the things in the room are in their right places. Only, they are a little blurred. Tamara floats here and there, she smells like lime-blossom tea. Gently, so as not to frighten her, I whisper:

"Tamara, darling . . ."

And suddenly she is close to me. Her voice cuts the mistiness like a knife:

"Are you awake? Do you feel better? Is there anything you want?"

I haven't the strength to speak, but I see my hand far off, a long hand that has grown thin. It reaches toward her dressing-gown, crawling along like a snake, the hand seizes the dressing-gown, feels it, touches the rather harsh material, and slowly, very slowly, the sensation reaches me. Tamara is maybe just a mirage, but her dressing-gown is real, it is there. And the hot tea that she makes me drink a little too fast, that, too, is real. I am no longer dreaming. Tamara is there. In the room, she is going and coming without the least noise, light as a flame. The rest of the house is absolutely quiet. Have I been ill for six weeks? Did she return from Italy?

"Are you there, Tam?"

That is all I can manage to say.

"Of course I'm here, little idiot! Be quiet, go to sleep."

Quite evidently, I am not dreaming. Reassured as to my mental state, I turn over and sleep.

Tamara took care of me for a month with what is usually called "an admirable devotion." She did nothing but that. For several days after my return to consciousness she forbade me to speak.

"Rest," she said. "If you begin talking again, you'll go off your head and say stupid things, you'll be feverish and delirious again. You've already caused us enough trouble!"

I supposed the "us" implied that my father had interrupted his trip simply to stand by my bed a few minutes each day, in profound silence, and to be ordered about by her.

"Now, René!" she would say. "You've seen all you should of her. You're going to make her want to talk, and she must be quiet. She's certainly not a pretty sight! And a man in a sickroom is like a bull in a china shop. As for you, my little red lobster, stop scratching your neck! Do you want to look like a sieve when you get up?"

Fever, weakness, and her kindly, scolding, and active presence all inclined me to enjoy a vegetative happiness. Around me, the room had changed, as if a storm had swept it. The old photographs, the dusty globes, the hangings, had all disappeared. A cleaning up had taken place which I perceived only through a semistupor when I had been aware of a great shaking of dustcloths, like wings, and the fine odor of dust had given the room a clean and white look, such as it had not had for a long time. Tamara slept there, on a camp bed brought down from the attic, and sometimes, when I woke up in the night, I could see the feeble light of her night lamp as she reclined on an elbow, smoking.

I was in no hurry at all to get well. Tamara was good and sweet. I was able to make my mind a blank and not think of anything. I foresaw obscurely that, as soon as I was well, I would have to face the same problems, I would again have to live in a state of uncertainty, I would have to work and reflect. But the days dragged by pleasantly now, in the sweltering heat of August. I did not even miss having a vacation. No doubt this was because I was very tired out, I would need to make up for years of insomnia. Every time I tried to have a serious thought, a kind of exasperated lassitude would overwhelm me, I did not manage to reason out anything precisely, and so I went back to sleep. Sometimes I looked at a picture on the wall, representing a tree-bordered avenue of cafés and orange-colored parasols, with rays of sunlight on the dusty road, the fresh green of the trees and the orange spots of the cafés being in the background. That picture, it seemed to me, put all summer before my eyes.

The first time I could really assemble my thoughts was one day when the doctor spoke to Tamara in front of me.

"This poor child is really unlucky," he said. "First, that fall from the trolley car, then this scarlet fever."

Fall from the trolley car? The words slowly filtered down to me. For a minute I seriously wondered how I could have forgotten that fall from a trolley car that I must have had. But I never took the rattling little trolley in Gers, I always walked, no matter where I went. So it must have happened somewhere else. Had I made a journey? Where? Suddenly I remembered Versaint. Was there a trolley in Versaint? Yes, but surely I hadn't ridden on it. Why that lie, then? A fall. A wound. Mechanically I looked at my arm. A long black-and-blue mark was still there. So that was it! The first words of which I was aware represented, then, one of Tamara's lies. I could just imagine how she had looked when she had replied gravely to the doctor's inquiries, "Yes, Doctor, the poor child really had a bad vacation," and then made that explanation. Her profile was serious and pure as a profile on a medal; I could imagine it, and indeed the same face bent over me night and day, as she gave me medicine or orange juice, as she washed my hands or let me sniff some Eau de Cologne. Her expression was the angelic one of a nurse dedicated to serving people condemned to death, and I

(211)

could not manage to believe it was just put on. However, one refusal, one awkward gesture of mine, sufficed to make the angel with the long lowered eyelashes turn, as if by miracle, into a she-devil.

"You'll take your medicine, or!" The unexpressed threat signified clearly something to the effect that: "or, sick as you are, I'll drag you down the stairs by your feet!" So I obediently drank the bitter mixture, and as she brought me a napkin and a cup of consommé, she became calm again, silent, assured, the modest but indispensable saint in uniform, bending, in her white apron, over my poor, perishable body.

At last I could eat a little, sit up in bed, and talk. Of the latter faculty I had no intention of making much use. Barely did I, from time to time, venture an affectionate thank you to Tamara, who always seemed to be carrying trays much larger than necessary, and basins so often that you would think I bathed night and day without stopping. And all she would say to me, if I did speak, was, "Be quiet, stupid child!" Then a mocking smile would flicker at the corner of her mouth, recalling the old days of confidential talks, days which I vaguely hoped would return.

Max came to see me when I had reached this stage.

"Greetings, you little pest!" he exclaimed jovially, as he entered my room like a blast of wind. His curls were disheveled, a wide grin was on his faun's face. He did me good; he was a breath of fresh air.

"You certainly gave us some gray hairs, that's something to brag about! Aren't you ashamed, catching scarlet fever at your age? And think of poor Tamara having to come back from Florence to spend her vacation here in the midst of basins and pills!"

"But why did she come back, Max?"

"What else could she do? To begin with, that idiot of a Julia sent your father a series of telegrams that were enough to make him think he ought to order a coffin for you. Then, you were yelling for her at the top of your lungs, you can't imagine how! If I'd not been at your bedside, you'd now be facing a reform school, my fair angel. And our beautiful friend would be facing a charge of having 'impaired the morals of a minor.' No more nor less. And complicated by another charge: an attempted assassination! If old Max hadn't been here to frighten off the servants and medicine-men, you'd have been in a pretty fix."

Tamara ran her fingers through his hair.

"Yes, Max, we realize you were a hero. I'll remember it . . ."

"Don't act like the respectful prostitute," Max grumbled. "I know all too well you'll remember. But you'd remember it still more if I'd not been here, I assure you. I must stop, I'm upsetting the child. Be seeing you soon, little demon. When you're well, I'm counting on you to do a series of drawings of your delirium. I could sell them under the counter, and we'd all live in great style."

Despite his pleasantries, he didn't seem to be gay, and went off, against my will, in a bad humor I didn't associate with him.

"What's wrong with him, Tam?"

"He's jealous because I'm taking care of you and don't see him any more," she replied with a shrug.

The explanation seemed improbable to me. Max had never been jealous of me in the past, so why should he be now that I was ill? Perhaps he had discovered that Tamara was fonder of me than he had thought or than I had thought? After all, this was possible, she was so good to me.

That evening I was again feverish, tossing and turning in my bed. She sat beside me and held my hand.

"Now, now, be calm. Go to sleep like a good girl. Do you want me to read something to you? Close your eyes."

She took an old book she had found in the attic and began to read in a hushed voice, sweeter than usual. The book, artlessly ornamented with garlands on the cover and title page, was called *Les voyages en Perse, Mesopotamie et autres lieux,* and the author signed himself as "the very noble Paron de Méré, great traveler and historian." She read:

"*. . . With him, I visited the Sultan's gardens, which appeared to be very spacious, perfumed, and ingeniously arranged. Among the shrubbery, trimmed to represent cupolas, were placed, here and there, minarets of graceful and daring form holding bells painted in vivid colors, and among the aviaries, which, I believed, were entirely of woven gold, the paths of fine sand formed sinuous curves which, they told me, when seen from the upper windows of the palace, formed words, comprising a laudation of the Sultan . . .*"

(214)

I cheated a little. From time to time I opened my eyelids to catch a glimpse of Tamara's brown face in the dimness of the room; her expression was serious and as if melting with sweetness, as she read in a lower and lower voice:

"... When they brought me a gold platter filled with divers sweetmeats, but whereon lay no utensil for the service thereof, I was nonplussed, and discreetly turned my eyes toward my host, who, in slow Oriental fashion, smilingly said, with great courtesy ..."

From one vigil to another, the Chevalier de Méré spun the tale of a palace servant-girl—whom he met behind the aviaries, the Chevalier being forced to leave the Sultan's palace before having completed her seduction, which he himself qualified as "daring and almost perilous," going off on horseback toward other places, and exclaiming over a series of flamingos and pink ibis in a swamp—until the time when I was just beginning to leave my sickbed and take a few shaky steps, leaning on Tamara.

"The way you've grown!" she exclaimed, looking at our reflections in the mirror. I had indeed grown taller, and I noted with satisfaction my smaller waist, my long pale hands, and my lengthened face.

"You must take some physical exercise and keep that figure. You are dazzlingly beautiful!" Tamara decreed. "I'd never have thought you could become so beautiful. You're going to be a sensation."

She, too, had grown thinner, but her face showed the lines of fatigue. Every time my father came into the bedroom, he looked at her sympathetically.

(215)

The calm evenings continued, with Tamara reading from the quaint old book:

"... *these creatures are worthy of a more ample study. I remained several hours observing them, making sketches, and I perceived that some of them could remain motionless on one of their long legs, which looked like sticks of pinkish glass, almost indefinitely* ..."

Two days after she had read that passage, Tamara gave me, to celebrate my convalescence and since we were going in for exotic things, she said, a pair of Chinese silk pajamas, which I at once put on. I had never owned such a luxurious item of clothing. I even hesitated to go to bed in such a marvel.

"Don't be silly, go to bed! You are certainly pretty enough to deserve to wear silk pajamas. It's extraordinary. Look, even your ankles are smaller."

That evening we did not accompany the Chevalier Paron de Méré farther in his golden palanquin. And since I was almost well and Tamara had gone to live again at the Rempart des Béguines, the unhappy gentleman remained forever in my mind standing before that swamp, in an eternal contemplation of the pink ibis.

XIII

THE ACADEMY did not open until October. I therefore
had more than a month of idleness ahead of me, and took
advantage of it to read a great deal and to make sketches
of Gers, from every possible point of view. Max deigned
to approve my work. But I noticed that he was more and
more melancholy.

"What's wrong with him?" I asked Tamara. "He acts
almost respectable, nowadays!"

"How do you expect me to know?" she said with a
shrug. "He doesn't know what he wants. He comes and
hangs around my place once a week, there's no getting
rid of him, and still he's not satisfied. He'll end up by
compromising me with your father, you'll see."

But there was something queer about her, too: she
seemed to be in a kind of serious reverie that made her
frown unconsciously, at times, and jump when I spoke
a word to her. She pretended that she was thinking with
regret of her interrupted visit to Italy. Max, when I
questioned him, took refuge behind similar embarrassed
reasons.

"I tell you there's nothing the matter with me, for God's

sake! My exhibition's not going well, that's all. Goddammit, stop teasing me, you're as persistent as a mosquito!"

I knew him well enough, however, to realize that an unsuccessful exhibition would only have thrown him into an Olympian rage, he would have let loose a volley of oaths, and there would have been a recrudescence of work. Whereas, instead, each day he sank deeper into a condition of mute suffering.

"Are you angry with me on account of Tamara?" I ventured to ask him one day. "Are you—surely you're not jealous?"

He raised his arms in mock despair.

"Jealous! Of that! Are you laughing at me, you little scarecrow?" And then he kissed me on the cheek. "You're stupid, darling," he added. "Of course I'm not jealous. I'm not even annoyed. You haven't anything to do with it. Don't worry about me, that's the best thing you can do."

I didn't understand. But since I could do nothing . . .

Even in the house the atmosphere was tense. The elections would take place in October, and my father, no doubt preoccupied with this, nervously paced up and down in his office, reciting fragments of his prepared speech, of which from time to time I overheard some eloquent passages:

". . . Liberalism is not, as some people pretend to believe, a compromise, a middle ground between the mummified Right Wing and a Left Wing too revolutionary to attract honest citizens. . . . It is the champion—the champion of a tolerant but firm position; it represents perfectly the civilized man. . . . The Liberal is he who resists inva-

(218)

sions, bending like the reed, but defending the intellectual heritage. The Liberal is a clear-thinking warrior, the standard bearer of moral values, and never shall we tolerate seeing the depositaries and transmitters of these moral values cheated in their interests. . . . They shall remain honored—honored . . ."

It all seemed to me singularly devoid of sense, as, indeed, did my father's ambition to "take part in the affairs of the country." And who, in Gers, could be considered as the standard bearer of moral values? My father himself? The Vallées? The Périers? How absurd! All the same, I was struck by my father's uneasiness. He was visibly distracted and worried about something. No one told me anything, everyone seemed to be sad. I almost looked forward to the fall term.

One day, it was the 17th of September, I was at Tamara's, lying on the blue divan of the first room. I was alone, waiting for her. She had gone uptown, on some errands. Through the window I could see the lake, a little grayish, a little yellowish. It was still rather warm and, a bit tired, I drifted into a reverie. A soft light shone through the ornamental glass objects. I wondered if Tamara ever enjoyed watching the light shine through those things. It seemed to give me new ideas about some of them. The little glass horse, for instance, with its sturdy look, its variegated coloring, its tail proudly held—you would say it was a horse for a horse show—he must feel, I thought, very sad on his chimney piece, sadder than Andersen's chimney sweep, for the violet and yellow light

(219)

shining through him was the very color of a sad stained glass window I knew, which depicted St. Nicolas, his aureole casting a yellow light, his bishop's miter a violet light, down upon the tombs in the cathedral. And the cage full of stuffed birds: it also seemed to cast a dark, funereal light. And the opaline lamp, usually so pure white, became, on the windowsill, a cloudy green like the depths of the sea. . . .

Could Tamara have read my thoughts she would have labeled them "childish." And it was true, they were childish. No matter what had happened to me, I still clung to childhood in many delightful, sentimental and superstitious ways.

I was absorbed in these vague reflections when I heard the key turn in the lock and Tamara came in, fresh and gay, shaking her hair, which gleamed with fine drops of rain—she had been caught in a shower—and, after throwing aside her beret and jacket, she flung herself down at last on the divan like a damp, freshly picked flower.

"Hello, darling!" she said, carelessly distributing some kisses on my cheek. Then she bounded up, ran into her bedroom, and came back with a towel.

"I'm late," she said, rubbing her hair with it, "because I spent such a long time with your father, choosing some new shoes."

"I thought he said he was going to be economical."

"Oh, economy's for old men, and I told him so!"

She threw the towel on a chair, looked complacently at herself in the mirror, then went on, "Say what you will, I have my good moments. I think I'm looking very well today."

And she did look younger than ever. Her recently trimmed curls, her face freshened by the rain, made her look like a college girl—perhaps just a little depraved. She began to search through the pockets of her jacket, which had been thrown on the floor.

"I brought back a little gift for you. Here it is."

It was a tiny silver letter opener, its handle in the form of a question mark.

"Isn't it curious? I found it at the Flea Market this morning. Your father thought it was pretty."

"Did you spend the whole day with Papa?"

My amazement must have shown on my face, for she began to laugh.

"Why, yes, the whole day. Just imagine! He wanted to relax a little!"

"Oh!" I couldn't think of another word to say, but I would have felt much more grateful had this little gift come from Tamara alone. Then I asked, "You went to the Flea Market?"

"Why, yes. And we lunched at his club. Then he took me to buy some shoes. And here I am."

I was intrigued by her look of satisfaction. Usually, time spent with my father put her rather out of sorts.

"At his club! You lunched together in front of the whole town?"

"As I told you. Anyway, it's not of the least interest. You see, don't you, that I'm in a good mood!"

With this, she began to prove it, without waiting further. Soon my clothes strewed the room, and I was just taking out my hairpins with a shaking hand when the telephone rang.

(221)

"Fool that I am, I forgot to cut it off," Tamara whispered, annoyed. She leaned over the edge of the divan toward the apparatus, dragging me along with her by the nape of my neck, and answered the call with me curled up in her arms.

"Hello? Oh, it's you! Wait a second." In an aside to me, her face shining with mischief, she said, "It's your father again!"

Decidedly, he was becoming impassioned about her. I did not listen further.

Facing the divan was a big Venetian mirror, another of my father's gifts, which Tamara had hung there, not without sacrilegious forethought. In the mirror showed a corner of the divan, with one of Tamara's naked feet pressed against my thigh.

"Why, what decision?" she asked in a slightly impatient tone.

I began to listen. My father was still talking. Suddenly Tamara started with surprise.

"Oh but, René, you're not serious? On the eve of your elections?"

What did he want? To go away again on a trip with her, perhaps. He must be completely crazy. I shrugged, ill-humoredly. He had always had the gift of intervening in moments when he wasn't needed, my poor father. Tamara, however, had become curiously gentle.

"How generous of you, my dearest," she said tenderly. "I never expected it, you know. No, don't come. I would rather be alone a while. . . . Yes, after the lecture. . . . Whenever you like, my dearest. . . . No, I can't describe my feelings. It's so marvelous. . . . I'll see you soon, dearest."

She hung up.

"Are you going away again?" I asked ill-naturedly.

Really, she pretended too much! That face lit up with tenderness, that melting voice, all those "dearests."

"Do you think you really have to be as nice as all that?" I asked. "He'll end up by asking you to marry him!"

She began to laugh.

"Why, that's what he has just done, darling," she said suavely.

She still had her arms around me, her brown legs still held mine firmly, my head still rested on her shoulder. Stunned, I did not move. The mirror still reflected two bodies pressed against each other, in a charming disorder of lingerie. I was about to raise my head, to free myself, to say something—and I fainted.

When I came to, my head was resting on her knees, while she was trying to get me to drink a little brandy.

"Hélène? Are you better?"

With difficulty I sat up, searching her face for a confirmation of what I had just heard. She smiled at me.

All of a sudden I began to tremble. The feeling of detestation that had just invaded me, at the memory of those words she had pronounced, "It's so marvelous," made it impossible for me to say a word, but I felt such a desire to kill, such a helpless rage, that she must have read it in my eyes, for she moved slightly away from me.

"Now, now, darling, compose yourself! You're not going to have a fit of nerves, surely! Hélène!"

(223)

She shook me by the shoulders a little, but it did no good. I still remained mute and was trembling uncontrollably.

"Drink a little. That better?"

"Tamara . . ." I at last managed to articulate. "Is it true?"

She smiled again that odious and tranquil smile. I clenched my fists in fury.

"Answer me!"

My voice choked on a dry sob, purely nervous. I could not shed tears. She took me by the shoulders and leaned me over to the right, toward the mirror.

"There, that is what is true, my darling," she said, in a voice she made low and tender, "you and me. Nothing will change between us. You know very well that you love me, that you will go on loving me, no matter what happens."

Her voice penetrated and moved me more than a caress would have done, and I was about to yield to her, if only for a few minutes. Then she made a blunder. "It will be like when you were ill," she said, adding, "Don't you remember how nice it was for all three of us to be together?"

In a flash I could see again my father's look of tender admiration as Tamara ran from the bedroom to the landing and back again, loaded down with pillows, medicines, thermometers.

Had she carried duplicity to the point of gambling on the results of that apparent devotion of hers? Or had she merely taken advantage of fortuitous circumstances? No matter. Roughly I disengaged myself from her, mechanically looking around me.

"Surely you're not going to murder me?" said she, again ironical. "Be reasonable, Hélène! Your reactions are always so childish! What good would it do you to irritate your father and me on top of everything? Listen, darling . . ."

I made an effort to speak rationally.

"Tamara, you are not going to do this! You don't love him, you've told me so hundreds of times. You haven't any reason to marry him. He will give you whatever you want, since he's so in love with you. But don't marry him, Tam! I beg of you! Wait a few days, think it over! You won't stay here all your life, you'll want to go away, you'll want to be unfaithful to him, you'll . . . Tamara!"

She shrugged, out of patience.

"Hélène, stop acting like a child! When you were sick in bed you thought it was very nice to have me live with you. There's no reason why that should be hateful to you now, all of a sudden. And even if it is hateful, you'll just get used to it, so there. Anyway, there's no question of waiting. Your father has just told me that it will be done very soon. You have but one thing to do and that's to bow to circumstances. I don't understand in the least why you're making this ridiculous fuss, since nothing has changed."

I tried to remain calm in spite of my increasing hysteria.

"But why, Tamara? Why? You don't need to marry him! He'll give you money, he'll take you for trips, since . . ."

Coldly she watched me struggling with my arguments

as I went on, "And anyway, I don't *want* you to marry him! If you don't refuse him, I'll *tell* him! He won't marry you, all the same, if it would make me unhappy."

"But you won't be unhappy," she said calmly. "Do you want your father to think you've gone crazy? You've talked so much to him about my good influence, there's really no reason for you to change your mind this suddenly."

"Why—"

"And if you were to give him a reason? You're sixteen, Hélène. Do you realize you might be sent for five years to a reform school? Or maybe to a convent—that would be more proper."

I was dumbfounded. She turned her back on me and went over to the table for a cigarette. Then, sitting on the arm of a chair, she said:

"Put your clothes on. And try for once to listen to me like a grownup person. There's no way you can stop this, get that into your head. People don't always do just what we want, in life, as you'll find out. I'm not going to give up a chance to get out of my difficulties simply to satisfy the whims of a little girl. For me, this is maybe the last chance I'll have."

Feeling crushed, I dressed myself. There was a moment of silence, then she went on in a gentle voice:

"I'm thirty-six, Hélène. For years I've lived without security. For years I've been wondering whether I'd die in a public hospital or in the street, or simply of hunger in a furnished room. I have no intention of hurting you, I swear it. And I have no intention either to renounce, for your sake, this offer your father has made. For me it represents stability and security. That doesn't mean a thing to you at your age. You can't understand that in a few years from now I'll be a derelict, penniless, without friends, without even the possibility of pleasing someone to make a living. I'm fed up. And if you only knew to what point I'm fed up, you wouldn't dream of protesting any more."

Already I did not dream of protesting any more. I had just come to realize there was nothing to do about it. All I wanted now was to leave, and quickly, before I should begin to cry, before I should again become weak. Tamara held me back as I stood up to go.

"My dear child," she said, "don't go away miserable like this. You know that I don't love your father, and that ought to be enough for you. I love you as much as I can love anyone, darling, and if I promise you that nothing will change between us, you know very well it's the truth."

She was almost imploring me. I looked at her with disgust. On that face I had loved and admired so desperately, that had been my sun, my horizon, the very incarnation of beauty, cruelty, voluptuousness and suffering, all equally delicious, there was painted that odious humility of beggars and of beaten women, that cowardice of irresponsible people, that same weakness that I had hated in myself and that she, unknowingly, had taught me to hate.

And she who, before, had lied with such superb assurance, without caring at all whether she was believed or not, how weakly had she just now declared that she loved me, confessed implicitly that she needed me!

I stood up to leave. It was beyond my strength to remain any longer watching this last and tragic transformation of

(227)

Tamara. She held out my coat to me in silence. As I went toward the door, she recovered her usual tone long enough to say:

"You may come back whenever you like, you know. You won't even have to beg forgiveness, this time. It will be easy, you'll see. Au revoir."

I turned to look at her before closing the door. She seemed to me almost ugly. She had not known how to vanquish me, this time. I no longer admired her.

XIV

I TRIED TO THINK of a way out. Desperately I tried to find a solution. No matter where I was or what doing, my mind was on this. At the Academy, where I was again attending classes; in the morning, as I got out of bed in my little low-ceilinged room; as I went down to the kitchen for my breakfast, running down the stairs to avoid seeing the dreariness of the empty rooms with their armchairs under yellow slip covers and their carpets rolled up waiting for the charwoman; and as I sat down at the marble-topped table to drink my cup of coffee that Julia served me with a distant air, I was still trying, eternally trying to find a way out. How could I prevent Tamara's marriage? That was the question.

Already half the town knew about it. At the Academy, whenever I passed a group of people, I heard their whisperings. I was "the pupil whose father was going to marry an unmentionable woman." Everyone looked at me pityingly. When, in replying to a question, I made some glaring mistake, or when with an awkward movement I upset my charcoal sticks or cupful of dirty water, I was not scolded as others would have been. My awkwardness was attributed to a profound despair. So they would quickly say, "Don't you worry, my child, it doesn't matter!" I rather enjoyed playing the role of hurt innocence. During the recesses, I knew they were talking about me in the teachers' assembly room, and I could imagine what they were saying. "Even so, a man has the right to live his own life," would affirm the Olympian Monsieur Lambotte, specialist in water colors. And the good *abbé* who taught "elementary perspective" would doubtless gently protest, "I don't contradict that, Monsieur Lambotte, I don't contradict it, but he might have considered the girl, he could have waited until she was married."

Even my classmates, whom I had considered so crass and narrow-minded, overwhelmed me with kind attentions, lending me their charcoal sticks, their crayons, a new textbook, correcting a bad line, and doing all this with a silent commiseration that astonished me. I had never thought that this event could appear so tragic in the eyes of the people of Gers, and I took wicked delight in realizing that this pity was an insult to Tamara.

Sometimes I met former classmates of Mademoiselle Balde's school, and it was obvious their mothers had recommended them either to be "very nice to Hélène, who's in trouble" or to avoid me with care as though I were already enveloped in the opprobrium that surrounded Tamara. Everyone obviously was eager to know about the wedding, the church where it would take place, the date of the ceremony, and I replied to their questions only with grief-stricken looks which all the town commented upon, adding to the general indignation, giving it a moral reason.

But evidently the hostile mutterings of society, which began to be audible, and the definite compromise of his election would not prevent my father from marrying Tamara, any more than would the "calumnies" being circulated about her and which he had not deigned to verify. What could I do?

The idea came to me that perhaps Max would help me contrive something to stop the preparation—already quite advanced—for the marriage. I telephoned him that I wanted to see him, pretending it had to do with my work, and as soon as he arrived in Gers I ran to meet him at Ford's Café, down by the harbor, where he had established his unofficial headquarters.

"Max," I said without further preliminaries, "what are you going to do?"

"About what?"

"To stop this marriage."

He shrugged dejectedly. "I've done what I could. She won't give in." His resigned sadness exasperated me.

"You haven't even talked to her about it, I'll bet. You didn't dare to! You—"

"My poor child, if only you knew how many times I've talked to her about it, begged her to reflect."

"It's not true," I cried, beside myself. I had hoped to find him angry, full of plans for revenge, ready even to reveal to my father his intimacy with Tamara. Instead, I saw that I couldn't count on him.

"It's so true," he went on after hesitating a little, "that I proposed to marry her, if she liked."

I was stupefied.

(231)

"And she refused?"

"Naturally. She said she wanted to be sure of the future, that she wanted to have a little security. That she would be surer of everything with your father. You see, I make a little money, but it might stop any minute: depends upon fashion. I don't represent any guarantee, as they say. Oh yes, she refused, and she wasn't wrong to refuse."

"So, you're going to let her do this?"

"My child, even if I opposed it, nothing would be changed."

"Well, I don't *want* this marriage!"

"Have you told your father that?"

"I tried to, but . . ."

I had indeed tried, but he had stopped me at my first words.

"My dear daughter," he had said, "in ordinary circumstances I would not have taken such a decision without consulting you. I would have considered that your happiness was involved as much as mine. But when Tamara, without thinking twice, came here to live so as to be able to take care of you when you were ill, she compromised herself to such an extent—she who had already been compromised by me—that nothing remained for her but to leave town. My esteem for her and my attachment to her are such that I can gladly repair this wrong which I involuntarily caused—which *we* caused—for by doing so I shall assure my personal happiness. You have always been very fond of Tamara. There is no reason why you should now, on a sudden impulse, deprive her as well as me of a satisfactory and agreeable solution. I understand your position with your classmates, and with the young ladies you occasionally see. It is perhaps uncomfortable. If you like, at the end of a few months, we can move to another place, go to a town farther along the coast. That is all I can do for you or all I wish to do."

From the sound of his voice I had realized that I would not be able to persuade him.

"So you see," said Max with a sigh, "you can't do anything about it either." And he propped his elbows on the table and stared at his glass of whisky.

"But we must find a way, Max! You can't let yourself be chucked out like this!"

"She told me she would see me as often as she does now."

"She said the same thing to me! I wonder how many others she's said it to. And you think it's true, maybe? You think it's possible? Then you're crazy, Max! She'll drop you, as she'll drop me and everybody else. She won't risk losing her position in society for either you or me."

I tried desperately to provoke some kind of reaction in him. As for me, I didn't mind being dropped by the new Tamara. This new Tamara, I didn't care anything about her, she disgusted me, this woman, this equal, this weak creature who needed a man, who needed my father and craved his protection. What I didn't want was to see her every day in my home, smiling at my father, entertaining guests, demurely ordering the meals, and dragging in the mire the Tamara I had so loved, admired, and also feared. No, I could not face the prospect of having constantly to confront my living memory of Tamara with this unknown person who would gradually usurp her.

Max could not understand me. As weak as I, and as

subjugated by Tamara, he was a man, and feminine weakness did not arouse in him any disgust. On the contrary, he might even feel that these signs of weakness in Tamara brought him closer to her; he probably entertained the hope of being able to console and comfort her if she were unhappy with my father. While putting first and foremost her desire for security, she might also not be insensible to this kind of love which he could give her. My efforts to arouse in him some kind of jealousy or property instinct were vain.

"My child, you're too young to understand Tamara's motives. You're sixteen, you can't imagine what it is to be thirty-five. You have no right to prevent Tamara from leaving behind her the idiotic existence she has been leading. Anyway, you'll see: as soon as she is more relaxed and is leading a more regular life, she'll be much nicer to you, and she'll be grateful to you for having let her do what she wanted to. You'll see, in the long run you'll be happier than before."

What I could not explain to him was that I did not want her at all to be "nice" to me, that in fact I did not love her any more. I felt I had been duped, cheated in some way. Our relations had seemed to me normal, admissible, almost natural, because of her virile energy, her attitude toward life. Her solitude, so rare in a woman, the contempt she had for the conventions and for the necessities of life as they are conceived in a small town, her poverty, even, made me tolerate anything coming from her, as I would have tolerated anything from someone who, risking his life constantly, should certainly be allowed to scandalize the neighbors.

Her way of "making an end of it" cheapened all her acts in my eyes, deprived them of their nobility and stripped them of all interest. But were I to explain that to Max, he would simply shrug. So I did not argue further. He would not do anything for me, he still loved Tamara. I would have to find some other way.

Meanwhile, time was passing and the date fixed for the wedding approached. My father wanted Tamara to lunch almost daily with us, and she did so. She had to be introduced to my grandfather, and he was invited to one of these luncheons, which turned out to be a memorable occasion.

In honor of Tamara, whom she adored, Julia had set the table sumptuously. There were flowers, the best glasses, and, on account of the darkness of the room, tall white candles in antique candelabras. Everyone was a little upset and ill at ease. My grandfather had turned up in strange attire—he was wearing a turtle-neck sweater—and bringing along with him his "companion," Madame Nina Péroul, who had not been invited or expected. In absolute fury against this person, who represented a living insult to his "fiancée," my father, in a trembling voice, ordered another place to be laid. After this bad beginning, my father made the introductions in a rather embarrassed fashion. Nina was a fleshy forty-year-old peroxided blonde, lavishly perfumed, wearing more warpaint than any Indian chief, but with a kind and trusting look in her big frog eyes. She flung herself upon Tamara, her kiss leaving a long red streak on my friend's brown cheek. My grandfather pretended not to hear Tamara's name, and after having had it repeated several times for him he asked, with an assumed air of innocence, "Soulerr. That's a Jewish name, isn't it?"

We tackled the soup in silence. Tamara was seated beside me, and from time to time she smiled at me maternally. My father observed us fondly, while my grandfather, absorbed in his plate, said nothing. Nina did the talking. In a raucous voice she emitted comments on the dining room, on the approximate price of the damask chairs and the pictures on the wall. Everyone ignored these remarks, and confronted with this lack of conversation, she resignedly poured out for herself bumpers of wine. By the time the meat course appeared she was broaching anecdotes of the most intimate kind, stories which, for my part, I did not find devoid of interest, but which my father listened to with averted face, his brows frowning threateningly, visibly torn between politeness and anger. Oblivious to everything, the good soul continued her drunken maundering, interrupting herself from time to time to arrange my grandfather's napkin. She seemed to be sincerely devoted to him.

". . . And in my time, believe it or not, I was one of the prettiest girls in the country. My looks soon went. It's not as easy as you think for a pretty girl to get along. In the beginning you see everything rosy. You meet handsome boys when you take a walk, they take you to the movies, they take you to the carnivals on the town square. In our town there were often carnivals, with merry-go-rounds. After curfew, they went round and round without music, so as not to bother anyone, and I remember the oily sound they made, like waves, and I remember how we drank champagne and then felt like making love. Oh, it was easy to earn a living in those days!"

My grandfather burst into a guffaw, and the poor creature turned her astonished eyes toward me. I said nothing
and she momentarily gave up. My grandfather kept on
eating, ravenously, and at times picked a decayed tooth
with one of his fingernails. Beyond the candlelit table, the
dining room was in darkness. The soft glow of the flames
lit up the big centerpiece of fruit, the white cloth, and
the company plates, scarcely touching the faces of the
people at table: they seemed to emerge from the darkness
and were silhouetted against the faintly golden Cordovan
leather walls. Through the French window at the end of
the room could be seen the garden terrace and the quiet
sky, dark with storm clouds, from which came no light of
any kind. Even the trees seemed to be painted in false
perspective. I became lost in my own thoughts and did
not quite listen.

Nina was now talking about a sister she had had a hard
time to bring up. I heard my grandfather declare, "Yes,
Nina was very devoted to her. Well, I ask you, what's a
young girl got except her looks to pull herself out of her
poverty? You must realize that, Madame, don't you?"

"Why—of course," Tamara replied, a little disconcerted.

Julia, who was serving the omelet and who was following the conversation, was flushing terrifically with the
effort of controlling her giggles. My father waved his hand
in protest.

"What's wrong, what's wrong?" mumbled the old man.
"Everyone knows about Nina and her little triumphs!
There's nothing to get upset about in that."

Nina, at this, burst into shrill laughter, as if someone
were tickling her ribs.

"You're right, Leo! I had what I wanted! It's good to be young! But life is short! Don't you agree, Madame? Now, though, I stick to one principle. There comes a time when all that's over, and you've got to settle down. Take me: I'm finished with all that stuff, now. Not even for some pin money, now, would I ever think about it, even. No more men for me. We've got to know when to stop, don't you think so, Madame?"

She looked at Tamara with her artless and rather wandering gaze and quite evidently without in the least meaning to be disagreeable. I almost burst out laughing. But I didn't have time. Bringing his fist down violently on the table, so that the glassware trembled and made a pretty sound of bells, my father shouted:

"Enough of your talk! Clear out, both of you! Without me, you'd both die of hunger, yet you dare to come here to insult me, in my own home! And insult my wife! Clear out! And you"—he addressed this to me—"stop pulling a face like that, or I'll send you next week to a boarding school where you'll stay till you come of age! I'm fed up with not being master in my own house! I . . . I . . ."

He was stammering and almost strangling with fury. Suddenly he threw down his napkin and left the room, banging the door after him. I heard him go into his study.

Nina, poor creature, had not understood a thing and was dumbfounded. After a moment's hesitation, Tamara also got up and left the room.

"All the same, there's no reason to deprive an old man of an omelet," said my grandfather, delighted. "Pass the plate, Hélène."

He took another generous helping as Julia hurriedly gathered up the mess my father had made.

I was almost thunderstruck, for I had rarely seen my father act as brutally as this, and it seemed to me a bad omen that this fit of temper had been unleashed for Tamara's sake. But I was still more nonplussed at seeing them both reappear, a few minutes later, and at hearing my father, in a rather embarrassed voice, excuse himself to Nina for his "nervous outburst."

Dessert was served.

"You see," said my grandfather, "René's like me. He's got real character! Violent! But good as gold. He's sorry right away when he flies into a temper . . ."

I looked at my father. He had flushed very red and was clenching his fists, visibly on the point of shouting again, of hurling threats and objects at that face wrinkled with malice. But Tamara held his clenched fist with her long brown hand.

"Well, Julia, let's have the coffee at once," said my father hoarsely. "I'm in a hurry."

As he spoke, Tamara slightly turned her head toward me, with a questioning look that seemed to say, "Well, what do you think of all this?"—as if she had just performed a juggling feat. Oh! I could still suffer. . . .

XV

MORE THAN EVER, now, I loitered on my way home, reluctant to leave the peaceful out-of-doors, the trees, the shops in the avenues, and brave the turmoil that feverishly raged, as I well knew, behind the quiet façade of our house.

Had it not been for Madame Vallée, who had not gone away for her vacation that year simply because she wanted to "look after Tamara," having nothing better to do, my father would have been in bad odor with the society of Gers. As it was, a good part of that society—all those who were not in the "Périer crowd"—had been obliged to send congratulations to my father, for the announcements had already been sent out, and flowers were stacking up in the great hall. Already the windows were decorated with long green boxes filled with geraniums, and, on each side of the hall, strange twisted bushes in earthenware jardinieres transformed the entrance into a kind of hothouse.

The windows had been stripped of their velvet curtains, and sunlight flooded the newly painted drawing rooms. Julia, her sentimental soul thrilled at the approach of the ceremony, was furiously polishing the brass, hanging new curtains everywhere, sweeping the rugs. Ever since Tamara had patted her on the cheeks a few times and called her "my child," Julia, whose precocious stoutness had made her used to being treated like a matron, was intensely devoted to her. I no longer existed for Julia. Affected by all this agitation, the charwoman filled the house with the hum of the floor polisher and the odor of fresh beeswax. The house smelled of beeswax and furniture polish, but there was also the harsh odor of new cloth and the slightly stale odor of damp linen being ironed. The office girls were getting their dresses ready for the wedding, which they would attend, and for the office luncheon—an idea Tamara had had, by way of making herself popular with the personnel. The chauffeur himself had offered to polish up the car during his idle hours. The house was full of workmen, and if I wanted to draw I had to do so on an improvised table, between house painters' ladders and beneath showers of plaster. My father wore an expression of smug satisfaction that infuriated me. I had not seen Tamara alone since our conversation, and she apparently hadn't even time to think about such a thing as she went to and fro between our house and the Rempart des Béguines, carrying some of her possessions from her apartment, discarding others.

In the midst of all this confusion I had only one thought, and it daily became more desperate: "What can I do? What can I do?"

The night before the wedding, I went into the room that had been my mother's and which had now been transformed for Tamara. Everything was there. The room was impregnated with a perfume that was too sweet: it almost resembled that of the Rempart des Béguines. Tamara seemed to occupy it already. Already she was established in it, with her disorder, her habits, that multitude of souvenirs that followed her with the persistence of iron shavings clinging to a magnet, her incomprehensible and deceitful charm. . . . On the low table were scattered her combs, her tortoise-shell mirror, the little black man of cloth which was her pincushion; on the mantel were the little glass horse and the stuffed birds, and near the bed was the opaline lamp. She had succeeded in making this room completely foreign to the rest of the house, a kind of independent domain that seemed to flout the somber and heavy opulence of Gers. The low bed, covered with an antique material, the bare white walls, the parquet from which the heavy carpet had been removed and which now shone with polish like the woodwork of a beautiful ship—all this smote me to the heart. This room was full of the gestures of Tamara, the gestures she would make tomorrow for the first time and which she would repeat for weeks, months, and entire years. I could almost see them in the air, crisscrossing, tracing invisible spirals, reviving that brusque and boyish grace of hers which, every time I saw it, thrilled me.

But I must resign myself to the fact that what I had loved had been only a delusion. I had loved her poverty— and Tamara was marrying for money! I had loved her cruelty—and each day it disappeared! At the rate it was disappearing it was possible to imagine her one day soon going in for philanthropy! I had loved her virile energy, to which I had submitted, and now she in her turn submitted and every day for the rest of her life would submit to that man she did not love. I had accepted the idea before. But that was when it only had to do with money for her immediate pleasures and because of the airy way in which she relegated those acts to the realm of tedious and trifling obligations.

But this! This, that she had wished for, desired, almost demanded . . .

I was standing there looking at the room, when I felt a hand on my shoulder.

"Don't stand there in the doorway, go on in," said Tamara.

I went in, and I looked at her. She was wearing a blue dress, open at the throat, and I could see that she had become plump in these few weeks, to such an extent that she looked very feminine. She did not speak at first, but moved some of the small objects about as if embarrassed. What did she want of me, still? She visibly hesitated to speak first, but as I stubbornly maintained silence, she was obliged to speak.

"You haven't come to see me for a long time," she said.

This indirect way of tackling things was likewise unusual with her.

"That's because I didn't want to," I said shortly.

"Rather, you were too proud to come," she said gently. "Isn't that it?"

I did not understand what she was getting at. She drew near me and spoke with assumed friendliness:

"That's why I thought you might not like to witness the

ceremony, tomorrow, and have persuaded your father to excuse you," she said.

What did this solicitude mean?

"Thank you," I replied cautiously. "But I believe I'll go, all the same."

"In any case, I don't want you to feel obliged to attend. Maybe, after all, it would be better if you did not."

"Better for whom?"

Quite evidently the idea of my seeing her at her "big wedding" was unpleasant to her. Had she also acquired scruples and feelings of remorse, suddenly?

"Why, better for everyone. For you, because it might distress you, and for all those people who would watch for signs of grief on your face and might hurt you with their questions."

I understood. My father and Tamara were afraid of the comments, already harsh, that were being circulated on my account, the remarks as to my distress, as to the scandalous fate they were meting out to an "innocent child," by their actions. Tamara was also, no doubt, afraid of a scene; for I realized all of a sudden that, ever since the announcement of the wedding, she had made efforts to prevent private conversations between my father and me. By fiercely refusing to fall in with my father's rare efforts at reconciliation, I had therefore played into her hands.

But of what was she afraid if, as she had stated, she was sure that nothing could keep my father from marrying her? In spite of everything, she was afraid I might disregard my own fate and make revelations to my father

(244)

that would completely overwhelm him and cause him to change all his plans. I realized in a flash that she was right. I had in my possession some short notes she had sent me during an absence of my father and which were of an edifying nature. But I no longer loved her enough to sacrifice everything to the pleasure of seeing her ruined.

"Well, what have you decided?" she asked, and nervously waited for my reply.

"I'll decide tomorrow," I replied with feigned lassitude. "At the last minute, I'll see if I have the courage to go that far."

I made as if to leave the room, thinking that, if she feared a scandal, she would call me back. I had reached the door in silence, when she called out:

"Hélène!"

I felt that I was in command of the situation, at least morally. If I could not break the marriage, I could at any rate torment Tamara. It was the first minute of satisfaction I had had since that telephone call of my father's had changed everything for me. I turned in my tracks.

"Yes?"

"Won't you come here a minute and sit down beside me?"

I sat down beside her on the bed.

"So, this sulking is going to last?"

"I'm not sulking."

"Then why did you refuse to come back? Are you so busy all of a sudden?"

She had taken me by the nape of the neck, as in the

old days, and I could not keep from trembling. She smiled.

"You see, you've not changed so much."

I freed myself, not without difficulty.

"Maybe it's you that's changed."

She pretended to be amused.

"What do you mean, changed?"

It was my turn to be ironical.

"A month ago, if I'd refused to kiss you, you'd have beaten me, wouldn't you?"

She made a threatening gesture and I jumped back quickly.

"Oh no, you'll not do that," I said. "You don't dare."

She shrugged. "No, because it would please you too much. Come, kiss me."

"No." I replied calmly, but without looking at her. I might have discovered that I still wanted her caresses.

"Come, kiss me. You know you want to," she said, sensing that my will power was weakening. But there was still another test I wanted to make.

"Ask it nicely," I said.

"What?" She stared at me in stupefaction.

"You can't force me to kiss you, I'd run away down the stairs. You're not at the Rempart any more, here. If you want me to kiss you, ask me to do so nicely."

I had forced myself to adopt her tone of former times. She smiled in spite of herself.

"Is this a revenge? I'll let you have it. Come, please kiss me."

I drew near. She kissed me almost savagely, looking me straight in the eyes.

"Don't pull such a face! You know you love me!" she said.

I had to lower my eyes. Near me, like that, she was still the stronger of the two. But I realized that she was afraid of me; the rest had not much importance. The game had begun again, but she would not keep the upper hand much longer.

As I left her arms I said, "I'll go to the wedding, maybe, after all. I want to be there to see your happiness."

I had the pleasure of seeing her turn pale.

The wedding morning was superbly beautiful. It was a day of mingled sun and wind, a bright, cool autumn day, "exactly in the right note," as my father declared.

It was an extremely brilliant wedding. Out of curiosity, the whole town had come to stare eagerly at the bridal couple. My father, in morning coat, seemed to be sincerely moved, and I noticed how he bit his nails as he listened to the staid little oration made by the mayor. Tamara, browner than ever in her light dress, kept her eyelashes lowered on her cheeks like a modest young girl—everyone agreed she was very good-looking. In the first row of invited guests, Madame Vallée fidgeted and simpered, having all she could do not to applaud her husband who, in his speech, was complimenting my father, and she feverishly nodded her head to mark her enthusiastic agreement. The room was densely packed with curious onlookers, among whom I identified some important business men, an attractive marine officer, Captain Arnaud by name, and Max Villar—he had avoided me, for we had not been on good terms since that discussion of ours—who was watching the ceremony with resigned melancholy. Monsieur and Madame Périer were there, gossiping in whispers, and Diana Robel, the young widow who had wanted to marry my father. I was in the second or third row, and when the newly wedded couple affixed their signatures, I could not keep back a tear of rage. It was at once lapped up by hundreds of thirsty eyes and commented upon by hundreds of malevolent tongues as the crowd left the town hall.

Mechanically I followed the crowd down the stairway. My father and Tamara reached the carriage, with their witnesses. I joined them.

"I think everything went off very well, my dearest," said my father to Tamara. "The mayor's address was very satisfactory, don't you think? And everyone thought you were very beautiful."

"I heard Madame Robel ask if you weren't pregnant," I said maliciously to Tamara. She shrugged.

"Hélène, your behavior is—" my father began, irritated.

Tamara interrupted him. "Let her alone, René. She did not intend to say anything spiteful. After all, such things happen."

My father smiled, a little astonished, already prepared for that final and banal adventure. I said nothing.

There was the wedding luncheon at the house, which lasted until late in the afternoon. Then there was a dinner, which I did not attend. I sat on my bed, calm, stupefied, not quite understanding what was happening. I was waiting for a feeling of suffering, I was waiting for tears, for a sudden irruption of real grief such as I had not yet felt. It did not come. Stupidly I kept asking myself over and over, "Will Tamara be happy?" Or rather, I kept wondering how she would spend this first night in our house, in her house, this night that would be the first of a series of nights, all alike. Would she not suddenly regret her lost solitude, her narrow bed, the disorder of the Rempart des Béguines? For a moment I hoped so, then again I fell into that state of aimless waiting.

At last I heard a great hubbub, doors banging, fare-wells, a "Good night, Madame," thrown out by Julia, and the sound of footsteps ascending the stairs. I stood up and half opened the door of my room.

"It all went off very well, don't you think?" my father asked, stopping on the way up to catch his breath. "And the Vallées were so simple, so charming! I did not expect everything to go off so well. But dear me, how tiring these receptions are! We'll sleep late tomorrow."

Tamara murmured something in acquiescence. There was a silence, then I heard her exclaim:

"No, René! Not in the stairway! Let's get upstairs first!"

And at the precise moment that she said those words I experienced a great feeling of relief. That intonation! It was the pretended indignation of a happy woman being a little outraged—I *recognized* it! For it was precisely my own intonation when she took me into her arms despite my resistance, when I would say, "No, Tamara, I haven't time," yet was at heart delighted with her tender violence. And strangely enough I thought of those savages who eat

(249)

the bodies of their ancestors in order, as they say, to inherit their courage. Maybe it did not have much connection with my situation, but that "No, René," pronounced in her languorous voice, made me think that perhaps Tamara and I had exchanged personalities. I seemed at last to have found the solution to the enigma. Perhaps I should have known the answer for a long time, ever since that scene in Lucy's Bar, when Tamara had gone so far that she could go no farther but must from then on renounce. This lamentable love of ours had been doomed that day, it had reached its limit. I was at last free. Even my former desire for revenge disappeared. It had been, after all, only a last attempt to revive the old tender antagonism that I was not to feel again for a long time.

On the floor below, a door closed. It must be the door to their bedroom. And alone in the darkness, I began to laugh.